A Horse Named Yo-Yo
A Depression-Era Fairy Tale

To Kelly—
Hope you enjoy the story.
Your friend,
Kyle
Psalm 33:17

A Horse Named Yo-Yo
A Depression-Era Fairy Tale

Kyle Nathan Buller

A Horse Named Yo-Yo
A Depression-Era Fairy Tale

© Kyle Nathan Buller 2012

This book is a work of fiction. Named locations are used fictitiously, and characters and incidents are the product of the author's imagination. Any resemblance to actual events or places or persons, living or dead, is entirely coincidental.

All rights reserved. Without limiting the rights under copyright reserved above, no part of this publication may be reproduced, stored in a retrieval system, or transmitted, in any form or by any means (electronic, mechanical, photocopying, recording or otherwise), without the prior written permission of the copyright owner of this book.

Published by
Lighthouse Christian Publishing
SAN 257-4330
5531 Dufferin Drive
Savage, Minnesota, 55378
United States of America

www.lighthousechristianpublishing.com

The story contained within these pages is humbly dedicated to the 2011 class of second graders at

Inman Elementary School

Other, but no less important acknowledgments go to my family, who have graciously helped in the editing process, supported me throughout my life, loved me unconditionally, and demonstrated the love of Christ; my wonderful friends, who have never let me lose sight of who I am; and everyone else who believed in me and supported me in my life and during this project, you know who you are; and last but definitely not least, my Lord and Savior Jesus Christ, the Author and Finisher of my faith.

Kyle Nathan Buller

Prologue: Early morning on August 22, 1918

The sun was rising, covering the landscape in brilliant colors, just as the soldiers finished the last of their breakfasts. Most of them just took whatever they could find from their packs, the small amounts of food they were issued barely enough to fill their stomachs. One of the older and more knowledgeable soldiers stood quietly near the edge of the camp, watching the beautiful sunrise. He was a man with a high forehead, deep sunken eyes, his face unshaven. Carefully, sitting down on a clump of dirt in the trench, he let out a long, deep sigh. Sliding his fingers through his dark brown hair, he slowly reached inside his jacket pocket and pulled out a small pad of paper and a pencil with a well-worn nub. Shifting his gun to rest on a pile of timbers, he took a moment to remove his glasses as he wiped away tears with his fingers. Then he very slowly put his pencil to the paper and began to write this long overdue letter, the words nearly flowing from the page in heartfelt emotion:

My dearest Sarah,

Words cannot fully express what I have experienced here these past couple years. There has been and continues to be so much sadness and despair, that I fear some days it will overwhelm me with the pure weight of it. Many of my friends have died, although I thank God I have not had to experience them dying in my arms. The same cannot be said for some of the others, I fear. Half of our army has already passed away because of sickness and disease, not even counting the ones who have been shot. It is such a burden, and it seems that I have been here so long. All I can do is pray that this silly, crazy war will one day end, and there will be peace on earth. I am at least fortunate that I have the friendship of what comrades the Good Lord has spared, to guide me through the loneliness invading my heart and soul.

One of the men I have become good friends with, his name is Tony. Since I used to have a dog with that name, we have become close friends. In the midst of battle, any bond you can form with a fellow is considered a good one. Why, just yesterday afternoon, we were reminiscing about home, and he showed me a picture of his girl back in the States. They live in Texas, on a small farm in the eastern part of the state. She is quite pretty, but don't you worry none, no beauty on earth could compare with yours, my love.

Anyway, he told me that they bought a horse during an auction to keep them company on their small farm. A man had to sell his at a low price. A horse! Can you just imagine? I should think you would love a horse to keep us company on our farm, or the farm we always dreamed about havin' when I return. He said the animal is so well behaved; it's like part of their family. I have read, as we have more time than most inside these trenches, that the bond between an animal and a human is stronger than any other. Anyways, I do sincerely hope you will consider it. If it is in Almighty God's will and purpose, I will bring a horse home as a gift, after this foolishness is all over.

Believe me when I say, I do get tired of all this awful fighting! All I hear are so many bad things, I ache for the times when we had the good things in life; sunlight, fresh flowers, hot, fresh meals. I know we have to endure these things for a time, but there shall be peace on earth once again, I am sure of it. In the meantime, there has to be another way to solve differences. I suppose it's just as well, perhaps someday. All I can do now is the best job I know how, under the circumstances. All I know is that I do sincerely long for the day when there will be no more war or fighting.

I know I have said it before, and it barely bears repeating, but I miss you so. Although I am surrounded by comrades within this trench, I still need my quiet time. During that time (it comes whenever I can find it), I close my eyes and pray to the Almighty for protection, with the special request that God would keep you safe. It comforts me greatly to know that we are both sleeping underneath the same canopy of stars. However, it is also with great difficulty that I attempt to sleep at night, with all the explosions and gunfire around me. I have taken to looking up at the sky and counting the stars. You really should try it sometime, it is quite the undertaking! I have lost count many times, but how I am constantly reminded of God's love and protection! Even here, hundreds of miles from home, in a foreign land, the same stars exist. I know that His mighty protection follows us both, no matter where you or I may go. Psalm 19 from the Bible is a great comfort to me, and I keep it deep within my heart.

There isn't a soldier among us here who I have not told about you. I have promised each one that they shall meet you. When we come home, we'll have a party and celebrate! They really are an interesting bunch. Some days I fear I talk too much about things, but when it comes to you, I simply don't care. I am so proud to have you as my girl. I wish you saw what I see in you. Every day I wake up, I have a picture of you beside me on my bed, which is nothing more than a hollowed out shelf of dirt in the trench. I kiss it every morning and do the same each night.

I can't help but hear the jokes of my men and I only wish they could experience what I have with you. Most of them are single and seem to have the world by the tail. If they only knew the beauty of true, unselfish love, they would think differently. My dear, the time we have together, however brief, is and has been, a joy beyond comparison. It pales only in comparison to the bliss that we shall have when we both enter the gates of heaven someday, hand in hand. I apologize if that may have scared you into thinking I am not coming back, but I promise I shall return to you. In the meantime, it is my sincere desire that when I do eventually pass from this life, God willing, it should be with you by my side.

Someday, I promise I shall take you on a tour through the French countryside, when it is calm, beautiful and untouched by the horrors of war. It truly is a breathtaking scene! In the meantime, I will send a small token of love along with this letter, hoping that they both find you safe and happy. In better times, remember how we used to talk fondly of our future together? I wish now, with all my heart that I was there to deliver this to you on bended knee, and how it pains me so, that I cannot. Just take comfort in that, the moment you put on this ring, I will be whispering vows of love to you.

This was my grandfather's ring, and now I want you to have it, as I know he would have wanted that as well. He would have been honored to have it given to such a radiant, amazing woman. Do not despair, my dear, I will see you again, and I promise you, we will have the wedding you have always dreamed of. I have already sent a letter of permission asking your parents for your hand in marriage, and they have graciously approved, and are excited to attend the wedding. Until the day I return home to you, my dear princess, may God protect you and keep you safe.

Your handsome prince,
Thomas

Pulling from his pocket the handkerchief that Sarah gave him just before he went away to war, he dabbed his eyes. He affectionately called her his princess because when they were children, he fell in love with her the moment they laid eyes on each other. He promised if anything were to ever happen to her, no matter what, he would come for her. He reached behind him and grabbed a worn leather book from his pack. He read it every night without fail; to remind him of her, but more than that, to remind him that hope still existed in the midst of all this chaos. It was a book of fairy tales given to her by her mother. It reminded him, as it had reminded her, that magic; faith, honor, and true love still exist in a world spiraling out of control. As he gripped the book in his hands, he set his jaw and vowed to find her. He imagined riding in on a white horse, or whatever color it was, and bravely rescuing his one true love. Somehow, someway, he would find her! With fierce determination, he closed his eyes tight, whispering that promise resolutely into the cool morning air. Next he folded up the letter; put the ring into a pouch, placing them both inside a small envelope. He had barely begun to stand up, when the back of his helmet bumped against something hard. Next, it flew from his head and landed in the dirt. Luckily, it had not made a sound when it dropped. It would be quite embarrassing to be captured by the enemy, or worse, after baring his heart and soul to his one true love. On the other hand, he thought, what better final act in life, than to express your devotion to your beloved before meeting your Creator?

Stooping down to pick up his helmet; he felt a cool, rough, slick object slide across the top of his head. Moving out of the way in surprise, mildly annoyed at this new disturbance, he ran his hand through his hair. Slowly turning around, he stopped to look up into the warm, gentle eyes of the most beautiful horse he had ever seen! This creature was a strong, deep chocolate brown mare with few markings, except for a single white streak running down his face. Thomas opened his mouth in amazement and slowly took a couple steps back, blinking his eyes. This couldn't really be! He had just finished that letter; surely this was a trick his eyes were playing on him! He blinked, but the horse remained still and lowered his head, to let Thomas pet his mane.

Reaching out slowly, he ran his fingers through the coarse hair. The horses' reins fell forward, to Thomas' outstretched hands, and at that moment, a quick, fleeting vision of Sarah, in a stunning white dress, flashed through his mind. His mouth fell open, his vision swimming with tears, as if he had just seen an angel. In that single moment, there was no denying what he must do next!

With one hand, he held onto the reins and guided himself up the ladder with his other. Occasionally he braced against the dirt wall of the trench, stepping on the rungs to draw himself from the ditch. His heart hammered in his chest so hard; surely the enemy must hear it through the sounds of battle! All around, his men begged him to stay down and hidden, but he knew he had a mission, one that none of them could understand. That letter crushed tightly in his fist, as he held tight to the reins, was his map, the worn Bible in his other hand, his guide. Taking a short rest on the ground, he managed to pull himself up, position himself in the saddle, sitting on the back of this animal.

Drawing deep breaths from his lungs, he looked around for a brief moment. He turned the animal back around southward and leaning down toward him, whispered, "I don't know where you came from, but whatever happens, I am grateful you arrived when you did. We need a name for you now; I reckon you wouldn't like it if I kept calling you 'horse' all the time. My grandfather was named Cyrus. It means 'young'. It comes from a king in the Bible who freed the Jews, allowing them to return to their home in Israel. Yes, that is a good name… I think I shall call you Cyrus." Glancing at the land around them quickly, he heard the shouts of the enemy and the rumble of tanks come steadily and ominously closer.

He recoiled in surprise as his eyes fell underneath a pile of brush. Peering through the dead, twisted branches, his eyes were drawn to a long, rusted, and worn cavalry sword. The weapon lay beside the lifeless body of a young man. Thomas cringed with anger and sadness, as he had no desire to know what had happened to the poor soul. He simply closed his eyes and said a prayer for the young man and his family. Stooping down, he took the sword by the handle and, after promising that he would finish what the soldier had started, he dug his feet into the flanks of the horse. With determination in his eyes, he spurred them both on toward their fate, whatever it may be, only knowing he had a wedding to attend, a beauty to rescue, and a promise to fulfill.

Behind them, deep in the trench, the company of men

looked around at each other, some of them puzzled, most of them scared, but all were silent. Others simply shrugged their shoulders, some walked in silence, wondering about this strange turn of events. But every one of them, every last man, helped each other out of that trench and once on sturdy ground, followed their commander at a distance. Their weapons were loaded and ready, not knowing where they were going; all they knew was that they couldn't let their comrade down and leave him alone to his fate. They were brothers, all of them, and as brothers, they must fight to the bitter end, whatever that may mean for them.

Chapter 1: The morning of November 7, 1929

Once upon a time, eleven years later to be exact, an unusually cool, brisk fall day dawned. An early frost blanketed the ground, covering a lone, rough, worn looking, furrowed field in a glistening blanket of diamonds. In the corner of this particular field, two men sat on an old wooden bench as they drank water from a wooden jug. Off in the distance, opposite the company, a horse was lazily napping in a shaded area beneath the barn.

Every once in a while, his coarse tail swished as flies landed on him, eager to annoy the animal and disturb the calm of the peaceful afternoon. Suddenly, a gigantic horse-sneeze escaped his nose as he stretched out his legs and stood up on his hooves. Looking around in amusement, he gazed out at the neighboring fields, noticing how especially barren they were. Clouds of different shapes and sizes flowed along the sky, reminding him of the wild mustangs he had run with in Minnesota years ago, where he and his owner had once visited.

This particular horse, named Yo-Yo, for curious reasons, leaned his head to the side to hear words carried on the breeze. The two men, who, just a few minutes ago, had been sitting calmly on the bench, were now in a somewhat heated dispute. "But you told me I had at least a few more weeks!" the younger man pleaded. Yo-Yo recognized the voice of his owner, Samuel. He was a caring, compassionate young man with deep brown eyes, one who knew the value of a dollar and would give you the shirt off his back.

The older of the two, a short, plump fellow with slight wisps of gray hair protruding from the sides of his head like antennae, wore an oversized, but fine, gray business suit. He stared at Samuel with an attitude of authority in his eyes, but his face portrayed compassion and his voice even more so.

"I am truly sorry, but in our hard economic times, we all must make sacrifices… maybe I can help to make it a little easier." Pulling another bill from his wallet, Alex, the banker, held it up in front of Samuel.

"Now, I'm hoping this will help you do the right thing… trust me, it's in the best interest of everyone involved, but it is my final offer and I am sincerely hoping you will accept it."

Samuel looked at the money sadly, and slowly let out a deep, resigned sigh. True, it was better than nothing, but the more he thought about it, the more he was tempted to call the deal off. Turning his head, Samuel peered out over the field, his eyes squinting against the sun, to notice a deep brown shape galloping toward him on thick, muscular legs. His last friend on this small farm, Yo-Yo had kept him company through many dark days, and many bright ones as well. Their friendship was very special and unique, and they both knew that the brighter days far outnumbered the darker. They could hold their heads high, knowing they had enjoyed a full life together.

As his friend galloped closer to him, his heart swelled in his chest as he let out a wide smile. But his heart was breaking, knowing what he was about to do. His thick, large hand rubbed Yo-Yo on the chin, as Samuel stared longingly into the dark blue eyes of his life-long friend. Warm, happy memories came back to him as he looked deeper into Yo-Yo's eyes, memories of buying him from a cotton farmer in 1919, as just a young colt, as well as memories of riding him around the back country roads and feeling free. And finally, Samuel's face darkened as he remembered what brought him to this terrible place, memories of his wife's mysterious and unfortunate death, and the poverty gripping them now, that would later be known through history as the Stock Market Crash of 1929.

 Samuel sat on the bench dejected as he rubbed his friend's face, Yo-Yo looking at him intently, equally as sad as he was. Finally, with a deep breath and a sigh of acceptance, Samuel stood up and turned slowly to the banker. Taking Yo-Yo's reins in his strong hands, he passed off his final possession of the farm, and his last, true and loyal friend.

 "Thank you Samuel… I know this must be a terribly difficult thing for you to do, but I have confidence that this time shall pass and we shall be made stronger for it. In the meantime, take the money I have given you and do what you will." Samuel sat back down on the bench slowly, put his face in his hands and cried quietly as the banker spoke. The longer Alex spoke, the more Samuel's shoulders heaved and sobbed, realizing what was about to be taken from him. Samuel slowly got to his feet, steadying himself, as the banker finished talking. He felt Alex's soothing hand on his shoulder as he led the horse away a short distance to say his last, heart-breaking goodbye.

 "Let's make this quick, I've got to get going, "Alex said urgently.

 Samuel patted his friend's mane softly and ran his fingers through his rough hair. A fleeting thought of jumping on his strong back and escaping, running as far as they dare, came to his mind. His better judgment got a hold of him though, because an old friend once told him that being a man meant facing whatever came in life, no matter how rough it was. He came around to look his friend squarely in the eyes and firmly took his face in his hands. He spoke one final time in a barely heard whisper, Yo-Yo's eyes intently looking into his, "I know I haven't been the best master, but I've tried to give you all you needed…" A ripple of fear and doubt came from Yo-Yo, in turn making Samuel shudder, from an unbreakable bond that only an animal and his master truly understand.

Samuel made a decision at that moment, whispering in a soft, strangled voice to his friend, "You may be going away, but I will find you someday, I promise. My wife has died years ago, "he said more to himself now. "I regret that I wasn't there to say my last goodbye." He pulled a letter from his pocket, reading it as he sniffed quietly. "I hope this letter will help me find her someday. If it's within God's perfect will, I will find you too. I will always have hope, you must do the same."

"I know you're scared", Samuel uttered in a thick, sad voice, once again staring Yo-Yo in the eyes, "Believe me, so am I, but just you remember those late nights in the barn, when I read to you from the Bible. It says in there that you should not fear, because the Good Lord is always with you. Now, I want you to do what your new master says, and don't do anything crazy," Remembering a quote from Les Miserables, he left his friend with a word of comfort, as tears streamed down his cheeks. "I set you free from all the fear, doubt, and uncertainty you face now and in the days to come, and I leave you in the hands of Almighty God." As he uttered these words, tears continued to roll down his cheeks and he was barely able to speak. A final time, Alex laid his hand upon Samuel's shoulder, and squeezing gently, walked away, leading Yo-Yo by the reins on a slow, lonely walk to the waiting truck.

    Samuel felt his knees buckle and his hands shook noticeably as he landed in the dirt, his knees bouncing off a rock, but in his sorrow, he neither saw nor felt it. The gate closed with a loud clang and the old brown truck started up, a thick cloud of smoke racing from the exhaust. As the vehicle drove away, Yo-Yo whinnied and stamped his hooves, another rolling wave of fear settling over him.

    Now almost a mile away, Samuel's thick tears threatened to swallow him whole as he grabbed deep handfuls of dust, crying wordlessly. Yo-Yo sensed the sorrow of his master, and he let out a thick stream of horse tears, sure that he would never see him again, knowing his master was surely having the same miserable thoughts. As these feelings raced through his mind, he hung his head and cried softly, as his big heart began slowly shattering into a million tiny pieces.

    A pickup truck made its way across a winding, twisting road, until it finally stopped at a flat sprawling plot of land. Parking the vehicle, the two passengers carefully got out, leaning back against the truck, hands in their pockets. After a short silence, they gazed out at the hand dug graves. As their eyes traveled back and forth over the cemetery, their gazes stopped on a freshly dug pit in the distant corner. Pointing his finger, the younger man nodded to his partner, "I think that one will work just fine." With hesitation in his voice, the other stranger said "I'll make the necessary arrangements," A large, muscular man with a deep voice, he set about handling the small knife in his large hands. Pulling two good size scraps of wood, and a length of twine from his pocket, he whittled them into well carved crosspieces, and put the two pieces together, forming a crudely made cross. Finally, he precisely carved a very important name into the cross, marking the grave. Holding up the hand-carved cross, he breathed softly as he spoke the name that had been neatly scrawled there,

'*TAYLOR*'.

Walking over to the grave, covered with a fresh layer of dirt, he whittled the end of the cross to a sharp point with his knife. As he slowly knelt down, he stuck it sharply in the ground at the head of the grave. Standing back up, he walked a few feet and stared out at his handiwork. Where the cross was stuck neatly in the dirt at the head of the grave, the rest of the grave had been covered cleanly with dirt. The two men looked at each other as the wind blew sharply across the graveyard, "So, who's that for?" the older man asked slowly. The next words spoken were cold and unfeeling, his gaze never wavering from the grave. Thoughts of what had just been done filled his mind. "You'll see, soon enough", the older man whispered as they walked back to the truck, the only sign that anyone had been there, a cross adorning a freshly dug grave, a fresh pair of footprints and a set of tire tracks, equally as unspoiled. The men turned once more to each other, the older speaking words of comfort to the younger; "You shall have what you desire. Ask and you shall receive." Making their way back to the truck, they slowly got back in and began driving away. They both smiled knowingly at each other, as the stranger turned in his seat to clap his friend on the shoulder. With a deliberate smile, the elder bored his eyes into his partner, "Yes, yes I shall." To the untrained eye, it would appear as if this was a gathering of two family members paying their last respects to the dearly departed. But the two men in the pickup truck, as it pulled away from the graveyard, knew there was so much more to the story.

Chapter 2: March 17, 1930

 The days passed quietly and uneventfully, slowly turning into weeks. Samuel eventually grew frustrated at the fact that his best friend was out there in the wide world with no one to protect him. He felt more helpless than ever. Trusting in God's plan was very difficult at times, but despite his frustration, Samuel felt an inner, unexplained peace about the situation. Still, losing his best friend wasn't easy. After months of grieving, he walked into town to clear his head. As he stopped by the post office, a sign hanging on a billboard announced a poker tournament that was to be played at the saloon nearby. With there not being much money to be had these days, the pot wasn't going to be very large, but it was more of a way for people to get their minds off their problems. The reward worked one of two ways, people could either wager what money they had, or any of their possessions they thought they would be willing to part with.

 Samuel ripped the flyer from the wall, and stuffing it inside his pocket, immediately went home. Not being able to afford to go in blind, he had to put in some real practice. Luckily for him, he was a fast learner. He contacted a good friend of his nearby, and asked for a favor. The man quickly came over, without asking any questions. Once his friend had got there, without saying a word, Samuel slowly picked up a deck of cards given to him by an old friend, and dealt them out. "Hey, now, wait a minute", said his friend, "I ain't never been a gamblin' type of man." As Samuel explained his situation, the man's gaze grew soft and he slumped his shoulders, "Ok, just this once, but you gotta know it goes against my better judgment." They practiced long and hard, all the different card games that people play, and they put most of the next days and nights in practicing.

"Thank you, Carl, I sincerely do appreciate this. I promise you won't regret it."

He had a desperate plan in mind. He was in dire need of a horse to farm with. Without one, he would be forced to give up his livelihood. But he promised himself that he would never abandon his search for his friend. An old comrade had reminded him once that dangerous times call for desperate measures. He knew that recklessness sometimes makes people act foolish. After they had trained as hard they could, during those lonely weeks, Samuel finally felt confident enough, at least, to make up his mind, and took matters into his own hands. Early one morning, throwing on a pair of overalls and a clean shirt, he grabbed a small cloth bag from the mantle of the fireplace, and set out on the half a day's journey to the closest town.

After almost six hours of walking, tall, gray buildings dotted the horizon as he sauntered to the edge of town. Soon, a decrepit, old sign, saying North Platte Saloon, came into view, hanging askew on its rusty hinges. As he walked up to the buildings, the citizens stopped whatever they had been doing, and stared at this newcomer. Most of them looked on in curiosity, but he couldn't help feeling a chill of apprehension as he noticed that most of the men, with their large forearms and thick facial hair, stood threateningly along the porch fronts, their arms crossed. Their icy glares seemed to burn through him as he hung his head down, careful not to meet their eyes. He wasn't in a mood to get into a fight today, unless he had someone's honor to defend. Then, that would be a different story.

As his head hung low, his heart hammering in his chest, he felt tiny beads of sweat form against his skin as he quietly moved his lips, breathing a prayer of protection. A few of the strangers mocked him, but he didn't care. He simply took a deep breath, turned the corner and just began to confidently make his way into the saloon, a frantic man on a mission. Just before stepping over the threshold, a thick, powerful arm shot forth like a cobra. A heavy hand placed itself on his chest, stopping him cold in his tracks.

"Just what in blazes do ya think yer doing 'round these parts?"
A tall, hulking figure fell across Samuel's line of vision as a hush settled over the town. Samuel slowly lifted his eyes, his gaze traveling over this beastly man. Large, thick calves led to a belly that was definitely not wanting for food. Massive arms, like the trunks of an oak tree, threatened to snap him in two at the slightest move. Deep chested, with a voice that could strike fear into even the strongest soldier, made Samuel shake slightly in fear. The sheriff's neck, which was roughly the same girth as his torso, tensed as a vein bulged noticeably. He roared in anger, "No trespassin' allowed!" causing those within earshot to tremble, holding their children close to them.

Samuel tried ambitiously to respond with confidence, as he knew any visible anxiety would blow his chances of doing what he came to do, and he couldn't afford failure now.

"I've just come into town here lookin' fer work, that's all. Not lookin' fer no trouble."

"Work, huh? There hasn't been no work 'round here for

quite a long while. Now why don't you start by telling us why you really come here?"

Samuel hesitated as his eyes darted around for an answer. He didn't want to give away his reasons for his arrival just yet, but it seemed at this point he didn't have a choice. His eyes landed on a healthy black stallion tied to the hitching post in front of the saloon. He placed his hand against the animal's mane, and with a voice half full of confidence, the other half, quiet fear, he chose his next words with extreme care.

"Please, sir. I'm in great need of a horse. You don't understand...I had to sell the one I owned, him and I, we was like best friends... " His voice trailed off as he was explaining his situation.

"Do you have any idea who you're talking to? My name's John and I am the sheriff of these here parts. Besides, this one here's my horse, and he ain't for sale." the man gruffly explained, turning on his heel to join his friends back in the saloon. Samuel's next words rushed from his mouth quicker than he could think, the fear in his mind threatening to overwhelm him, jumbling his thoughts.

"Please, I got just a little money, it ain't much at all, but I can deal with the best of 'em", he said with as much confidence as he could muster.

"You think you can play against me?" the sheriff scoffed, confident that he could win, even with his eyes closed. "Suppose that's fair enough. Can't say I've had too much experience, but it'll be plenty, I assure you. Name your game, stranger," the sheriff sneered.

Samuel thought for a moment and said the first thing that came to his mind, "I played enough to get the idea. I don't know a lot, but it'll be enough. Like ya said, you're the sheriff, whaddya suggest?" The sheriff slowly smiled, the corners of his mouth turning up in a sneer. This was going to be much easier than he thought. "Uh, how about 7 card stud high. Winner takes all. Whaddya say about two outta three games?"

"Sounds good enough", Samuel said, shrugging his shoulders. Even though his voice was hesitant, he tried to maintain a certain amount of confidence in his hastily learned abilities.

John walked over to an empty table, and picking up a large cloth bag, undid the drawstring and dumped its contents out on the table. Betting chips rolled all over the surface. Gathering the chips, he put them into nice, neat piles. Next, he grabbed a deck of cards, pulled up a chair and grunted as he sat down, his old age creeping in. Samuel sat down in a chair opposite the sheriff. Squinting through his eyes up at his opponent, John hit the corner of the pack on the edge of the table, the deck falling out uniformly, his eyes never leaving his opponent. The sheriff separated the deck into two piles and stared down at them for a minute. Lowering his hand to his belt, he brought forth his revolver from his holster and laid it on the table, the barrel pointed to the left, toward the door of the saloon, between the two men.

"Wait a minute, just what is that? That wasn't in the deal", Samuel asked hesitantly, trying his best not to betray his fear.

"Let's just call it insurance, shall we? We really can't afford to have any cheaters. All of us here gotta play fair.", he smiled slowly, "Now deal."

John had a hunch that this man knew a bit more about the game than he was letting on, and he wasn't about to take any chances.

Samuel couldn't understand how threatening a newcomer with a weapon was "fair", but he wasn't anxious to argue the point. Maybe the sheriff was suspicious about his playing ability, and rightly so, but still... threatening him with a gun? Breathing deeply, he simply took the top card from the pile and was just about to deal, when the sheriff whistled loudly. Instantly, five men came to his side, their swaggers showing they either meant business, or were too drunk to care. In either case, they could be dangerous. John yelled triumphantly, "Welcome to the tournament, boys!" Before the cards were dealt, each player made their initial bet. Grabbing a couple of chips, Samuel spoke up first in a quiet, confident voice. "I bet 5 dollars. That's all the money I got. If I win, I get the horse," he said staring at the sheriff, nodding his head to the door of the saloon. "But if I lose", now his voice deepened and slowed, "you can have all the money I have left, plus whatever else is put on the table. I'm already so poor; you will have stolen everything from me. I got almost nothing to lose." Each of the other players, now realizing the seriousness of this game, began to make their bets in turn. Samuel started to awkwardly deal the cards to his opponents, struggling in his mind, to remember the rules of this particular game. He began playing their game, knowing it would take more than luck to get through this. Samuel brought his hand up and slid it across his forehead, wiping away sweat, as he turned his card up. A blonde haired fellow named Marshall let out a disappointing grumble as he made a bet of ten cents. A wiry fellow, a man named George, stood up as he slammed his cards down on the table, "I fold", he said, slowly standing up from the table and walking away, but not before he walked past the sheriff, leaning down to whisper into his ear.

"You win this, and I'm buying the drinks tonight."

"Ya got a deal", the sheriff clapped his friend on the back, then yelled, "Looks like drinks on the house for everyone!" A rousing cheer rose from all the patrons.

"Alright, let's get back to the game", Samuel stated impatiently.

Instantly, the other men reached down and brought their guns up, laying them on the table in a threatening manner. Samuel's eyes darted nervously between the weapons, and the men stared up at him in a challenging manner, and he slowly swallowed the lump forming in his throat. 'Maybe it would be best if I just stay low', he thought wisely. The play continued, with one of the next opponents calling their bets. Play continued as the rest of the opponents slowly raised the stakes. Samuel was aware that these men meant business. His brow furrowed in concentration as he stared at his cards intently.

The round ended with the sheriff again, dealing each player a seventh and final card, completing their hand. He whispered softly, his eyes becoming slits, never leaving Samuel, "I raise ya 5 more dollars." 'What are you doing?! That is an outrage!' Samuel nearly pleaded, the sweat forming rivers down his neck. Surely, by now, they could see his fear. He didn't have that kind of money! Then he remembered. His late wife's wedding ring was the only thing he owned, that could possibly keep him in the game! Now that Yo-Yo was gone though, he wouldn't even think of parting with it! Ever since she passed away, it was the only memory of her that he had to hang on to. He pressed his hand to his pocket, making sure the ring was still there, when his fingers wrapped around the familiar shape. He'd do anything to honor her memory, and knew without a doubt that she would have wanted him to be happy. He decided then and there that maybe, just maybe this was what she would have wanted him to do after all.

Suddenly, he felt a sharp twinge of guilt, as memories of his wedding day flashed through his mind. With a deep sigh of remorse, he closed his eyes, and whispered, "I'm so sorry, but I don't know if there's another way outta this. Someday I pray you forgive me for what I'm about to do." As he whispered to himself, he did his best to ignore the pangs of regret. Closing his eyes; he reached his trembling fingers into his pocket and slowly brought it out. The eyes of the men surrounding him widened as he pulled the ring from his pocket. As they looked on, his palms got sweaty as he fished the ring from his pocket. The small voice of level headed reason inside Samuel's head whispering, "Don't do this! This can't end well! Doesn't it mean anything to you?" The ring definitely did mean something to him, but he was sure she would have understood and been on his side, had she been alive and here with him now. And so, ignoring the pleas of his conscience for the final time, and with the ring clutched tightly in his fist, he slowly lowered it to the table and opened his palm, the clink of the metal against the table sounding just as empty and hollow as his heart felt now.

"Well, look at what we got here", the sheriff eagerly said, in a voice loud enough for all the customers of the saloon to hear. Instantly Samuel's hand reached down as he tried to wrap his fingers around the ring, regretting his decision.

"Remember now, you brought it to the table, no taking bets back." John warned as he reached over and gripped the handle of his revolver, sending a clear message to

Samuel. A dark skinned woman snatched up the ring after the sheriff had set it back down on the table, smiling as she placed it on her finger. "It aren't fer you", John bellowed. The sheriff quickly grabbed it back from the hand of the young woman.

"Now if you'll excuse us, we got us a game we need to finish", John warned the woman again in a gruff, authoritative voice. As she turned and left the table roughly, the other men simply stared her way, smiling goofily. At the same instant, Samuel turned his head as a coughing fit came over him. As their heads were turned, John took the opportunity to snatch Samuel's cards from where they lay on the table and substituted them for lower cards, giving Samuel a weaker hand! As his buddies' heads were turned, they called out to the woman, while Samuel went up to get a drink of water. John took that opportunity to switch out the rest of his opponent's cards, his hands working quickly as if he had had plenty of practice. When he had finished, they all held lower cards in their hands. Samuel turned back forward, apologizing for his coughing fit, as the other men turned around as well. As they were distracted, John's hand shot back to his cards as they continued the game, no one any the wiser.

Starting with Samuel, all players proceeded in a counterclockwise direction again. Samuel took all seven of his cards, and laid them down on the table. In a disappointed voice, he said, "Looks like I got the short end of the stick. One pair." Marshall took his turn next, not speaking, as he carefully revealed his hand, two pairs. The rest of the players each laid down their hands, none of them saying a word.

John, the sheriff, laid down his cards. Grinning from ear to ear, he said victoriously "Looks like we got us a winner!" Greedily, he reached for the chips. Just as his fingers grasped the ring on the table, Samuel batted his hand away quickly, in protest. "Haven't finished the game yet," Samuel said slowly, in his best cowboy impression. All of the men stood up at the same instant, cracking their knuckles as they walked toward him, a couple of them picking up bottles. As they threateningly moved toward him in a close group, his eyes focused on the nearest man, Marshall.

In two wide strides, the assailant broke away from the rest of the group and rushed at Samuel, flinging the empty bottle at his head. His momentum had carried him too far though, and the bottle crashed into the nearest wall as Samuel ducked and bounced up to shove his hands hard into the man's chest. He clutched the collar of Marshall's shirt roughly as he propelled them both backwards, sending Marshall flying over the counter and landing in a heap. Instantly, the second attacker, George, followed behind him, his fist connecting with Samuel's shoulder as he staggered forward in pain. As it was only a glancing blow, Samuel still had the awareness to wrap his leg around George's, tripping him, sending him sprawling to the ground. Samuel fell down to the ground in a heap, with George, holding his shoulder as the slim faced gentleman of the group, called Anthony by the sheriff, pulled a large knife from a holster in his belt and held it out menacingly, prepared to attack!

As a young teen, he had gotten in many fights in the schoolyard with kids, mostly bullies who were tired of what they thought of as his "goody two shoes attitude". His humble, generous, caring personality that so irritated the bullies, was an outward result of him accepting Christ years earlier. That decision was the only thing he had ever known, as it had happened rather early in his life. But as a result, he was made fun of and given the nickname, "Preacher Boy". He didn't care much, though. He knew that in him was something greater than what was in the world. In an attempt to get away from the bullies, he fell in with another, very different group of young boys. Most of them were sons of missionaries, so at first, he felt comfortable with them. But the more time he spent with them, the more they began talking about going overseas and spreading the gospel. A very noble endeavor indeed, and he would have gone with them, had it not been for something that would change his plans.

One day, after buying some food from a man in town, he went home to eat. Soon after, he developed an unusually high fever. Also, he had headaches that once in a while got so terrible he could barely stand them. His mother rushed him to the doctor and he was diagnosed with polio. After weeks of pain, his right leg became paralyzed and he couldn't move it even if he had wanted to. This led eventually to a slight limp that would be part of him the rest of his life. He knew then that his plans to go overseas were gone. After weeks of resting, he became angry at God for not allowing him to preach the Gospel. His mother graciously tried to cheer him up by inviting missionaries over and letting them tell of their experiences, but in his anger, he just pushed them away further. Soon, the visits became less and less.

Many nights, he would ask God why this was happening to him. His mother had left a Bible on the dresser, hoping he would open it and find comfort for his grief. After staring up at the ceiling the next few days, he began reading the Bible every night. He discovered that suffering led to perseverance and courage. After many nights of prayer and patience, one morning, a miracle occurred. He discovered he had no symptoms anymore, they just miraculously disappeared. No headaches, no fever, nothing! After a few more weeks of making sure his symptoms really were gone, his mother sent him back to school, but still a slight limp would remain the rest of his life. He thought the beatings from the bullies would stop, but they continued as if Samuel never left. All he thought about was what he had read, about suffering leading to determination and bravery. So, he took the punishment and beatings without too much of a fight. Although, once in a while, he was forced to fight back, especially when the bullies talked bad about his parents or someone close to him.

As a result, he became more and more skilled at learning to stand up for himself, through violence if necessary. But he tried to avoid that route, if at all possible. That memory affected the way he viewed his faith the rest of his life. He was more than willing to defend himself when it came to God, but his was a quiet, private interaction between him and his Savior. Needing to depend on others was beyond him, he believed. Whenever the bullies would ruff him up, he tried and tried to stand up for himself, but he never was really able to give them a reason for what he believed and why he believed the way he did. He had been saved so early in life that he never really had an experience that forced him to question and strengthen his faith. Sadly, as a result, even though his faith was genuine, it was gently slipping from his grasp, into the realm of a childhood fairy tale. But soon, all of that would begin to change.

His feet planted, he was fully prepared to defend

himself. Convinced now that these men wouldn't be too willing to listen to reason, Samuel saw Anthony thrust the knife toward him, a wild look in his eyes! Samuel turned aside at the last possible instant, at the same time his hand snaking out, and tightly clamped down on Anthony's wrist. He tightly held his attacker's wrist and squeezed against the nerves, causing Anthony to grimace in pain, his hand opening as the knife started to clatter to the floor. Taking his foot, he kicked the knife away from Anthony, as it seemed to hang in mid-air, watching as it tumbled end over end. Landing hilt first, its blade embedded in the ground just outside the doors of the saloon. Two of the three remaining men came rushing at him from either side. Samuel screamed in pain as his arms were jerked behind him roughly, pinning them behind his back. He struggled fiercely as the other man came rushing toward him, fists flying. His body jerking from side to side, Samuel tried to avoid the blows, but still some of them connected. Using the strength in his back and shoulders, he flung himself backwards and caught the man who had him in a bear hug, off guard. The man holding him lost his balance, his knees buckling as they went down together in a heap. Both their bodies landed awkwardly atop a table, the excess weight breaking it in two. Samuel brought his elbow down and struck his opponent's chest, knocking him out cold, as his head landed and hit the hard wood floor with terrible force.

Gingerly nursing his injuries as he stood up, he looked around to see the last man bolt for the door, apparently in no mood to face any more humiliation. It was just as well. Even he didn't think he could take on anyone else now, not in the shape he was in. Wheeling around, Samuel heard a familiar, frightening voice bellow deeply, "Get outta my saloon now! I don't wanna see your face around here again!" John screamed in rage. Walking over to the card table, he slowly knelt down and began to pick the ring off the floor, when a boot slammed down on his hand, causing him to scream in agony. John knelt down and picked up the ring, at the same time, held his gun out, the barrel pointed directly at Samuel's head! "I'll be takin' that", the sheriff said in a low, threatening voice" I could give this to someone who really deserves it. Now, just take your horse and leave, and never come back!"

Samuel moaned in pain as the sheriff turned on his heels and walked out of the saloon. The rest of the patrons were too scared now to do anything, as they went back to minding their own business. After a few minutes of rest, Samuel hobbled to his feet and slowly left the saloon. Once outside in the cool air, he leaned back against the door frame, breathing heavily. As he recovered slowly, he thought about the events that had just occurred. The realization of it all crashing down on him like the blow of a sledgehammer, he slid to the ground slowly. Putting his fist to his mouth in horror, tears fell down his cheeks. He never meant it to end like this! Not only did he gamble, an act which he would have never even considered otherwise, even if it was to get what he needed, he gambled away one of the things that meant the most to him. Whispering in futility to the sky, his body shaking, "I'm so sorry..." his tears falling harder down his cheeks.

Standing up on weak legs, he staggered over to the hitching post, roughly undoing the rope that held his new horse and slowly mounted the saddle. At the instant he swung into the saddle, the horse reared up on its legs, forcing Samuel to hold tighter to the reins, his knuckles turning white from the strain. The horse's eyes widened in fear as Samuel fought to keep him under control. "Settle down, boy!" Samuel ordered the horse. Pulling sharply against the reins, he finally managed to bring the horse down on all fours. Patting the horse on the neck, he breathed a sigh of relief.

Very cautiously, he mounted the horse again, pulling back against the reins gradually and bringing the horse to his feet. He was abruptly jerked though, as the mount turned around, facing toward the saloon. The street ahead of him was full of people passing back and forth, and children playing in the streets. With a loud whinny, the horse, rightly named Malice, pawed at the ground and took off like a bullet from a gun, into the thick crowd of people. Frightened faces turned their way as children and mothers dove for safety. Samuel tried hard to change the horse course, but it wasn't about to listen. As a young boy and girl passed the street, Malice reared up on his hind legs and flailed his front hooves wildly, nearly striking them both in the head, if it hadn't been for Samuel's quick thinking. Yanking hard on the reins, the force caused Malice to turn his head sharply aside, avoiding the children by mere inches.

As the townspeople struggled to move aside, Malice leaned down his head, staring down the street. Letting out a snort, he flew past the post office and the stables. Samuel struggled to hold on, the wind whipping past him as Malice's mane flew behind him. Samuel's body jostled back and forth, reminding him of his injuries. Just ahead, a Model A Ford was bearing down on them from the other direction. With people crowding both sides of the street, Samuel groaned. They were about to collide with the vehicle and nothing could be done!

As horse and rider galloped closer to the car, Malice

dug into the ground with his feet and pushed off, sending them jumping over the vehicle, as if it was a fence! They sailed over the car cleanly, as the driver grew pale with fear. The passengers inside looked on in awe as the horse leaped over them. Samuel held a hand to his side as they came down with a jarring thud. As the saloon came within sight again, Samuel breathed heavily, wanting to just get off this horse! Several more loud whinnies came from the horse, as Malice screeched to a halt in front of the saloon. Samuel loosened his grip on the reins and tumbled into the street, nursing his injuries.

"Unhh", muttered Samuel, rolling around in pain.

Samuel just barely heard a loud gruff voice yell from inside the saloon, "What is the meaning of this?" the sheriff bellowed. A drinking glass crashed against the wall of the saloon, and moments later, a giant, hulking figure came out into the light. John reached back to place his hand around the grip of his weapon. Samuel shielded his eyes as he gingerly got up on his feet. Drawing in deep breaths, he stammered, "Sir, I tried to take him back to my place, seeing as how I rightfully won him, but he ain't having any of it! He put up quite a fight, trying to get back to this saloon."

John sauntered up to Samuel and Malice, and without uttering a single word, drew back his hand, slapping Malice roughly across the face! Anger in his voice, his face red, John screamed, "What are you doing back here, you stupid animal! Go on! Get outta here before I teach you a lesson!" Malice stared back at him sadly, failing to understand what he had done to upset his master, as John slapped him again! The sheriff spoke further, his voice seething with rage! "You and I used to be friends, but we've had our fun, don't you see? It's over now! You're nothing more to me than just a dumb creature! I don't care about you! I was just using you to get what *I* want! You saw the same things I seen, you were right there with me when I done the things I done, you're just as terrible as I am!" He turned to Samuel now, "I only told you my horse wasn't for sale to get you in on the card game. He still ain't, but I needed a way to lure you in." Samuel eyes drooped as he finally understood. "I really don't care two bits what happens to him.", he said, pointing at Malice. "I won fair and square and you lost this", he said, pulling the ring from his pocket and holding it up dramatically. His voice shaking, John drew back his hand, and slapped the poor animal again! Samuel screamed helplessly, "Please stop! Don't hurt him!" as he clamped his hand over John's wrist, preventing him from hurting Malice further. "Get outta my way, boy! I am the law here! I make the rules!" John's words slurred, clearly he was drunk. Yanking his hand away, John reached toward the hitching post, grabbing a wicked looking leather whip!

    His eyes wide and bloodshot, John drew back the whip and let it fly toward the helpless animal! "NOOOOO!", Samuel screamed jumping heroically at the last instant in front of Malice. Shielding Malice from the coming blow, the sharp sting of the whip caught him squarely on the side! His body crumpled to the ground as he screamed in pain. Very slowly, he placed his hands against the wood platform and got to his feet. Samuel stared at John defiantly and wrapped his hand around Malice's bridle. He moaned in pain as his side throbbed. His next words came slow and purposefully, as he struggled to catch his breath. "This horse may not... be the tamest horse... around, he may be likely to... go off and do his own thing, but that gives you no right to treat him the way you did! No animal ...or person for that matter deserves that kind of treatment!" With each word he spoke, he winced in pain. "I'm gonna... do you a favor. I'm taking away your horse for you ...just like you wanted! And he's coming home with me, just like we agreed! ...He's precious, and somehow he's gonna prove to you his worth! I know you think he ain't capable of much and may even be useless, but he aint! One day, he's gonna show you! He's mine now!" Limping over to Malice, his muscles screaming in pain, he gingerly mounted the horse, placing his feet in the stirrups.

Slowly Samuel leaned down to rub Malice's head and neck, calming him. After Malice let out a few friendly snorts, he stayed still for a while, not wanting to leave the sheriff. Nearly forcing the animal to turn around, Samuel leaned down to whisper slowly, his voice trembling, "This isn't the way I meant for any of this to happen. It wasn't supposed to end like this..." Slowly, they made their way to Samuel's homestead, as Malice fought to return the whole way home. As his shoulders slumped, head turned down, the tears were falling from his face in rivers the entire journey back.

During their long journey back home, Malice fought harder and harder the closer they got. Along the way, thoughts of what he had done during the tournament weighed heavily on him. In desperation, he had done things he never expected to ever do. He had gambled, something that was totally against his character. Then, to defend himself, he got in a fight with some very rough men, men who were led by a corrupt sheriff. When he thought of the sheriff and the showdown with him and Malice, chills snaked down his back. There was something awful wicked about him.

    Inside the saloon, John stared out into the street, his hands balled into fists. His breathing came in ragged gasps as he watched Samuel and his horse disappear over the ridge. They had nearly set up the tournament perfectly! He couldn't care less about losing his horse though! "Good riddance, Malice! At least I came away with something," John said to himself, opening his hand to stare at the simple wedding ring. Samuel didn't suspect a thing, at least not yet. The farmer had a deep love for his friend, John knew. Alex told him as much, and John knew better than most that love is blind. As long as Samuel kept up the search for his horse, he would remain completely clueless as to the events swirling around him. John felt like a powerful story was being written here, each person involved, a page; each event that occurred, was a chapter that deepened the conspiracy.

Chapter 3, March 18, 1930

After Samuel and his new horse got back to the farm, Samuel said to him, "I gotta keep ya now. I want you to realize you're worth more than you know. I don't know where life will take ya, but somehow I pray you have the opportunity to prove yourself. Now, let's see what kinda prize I got." He knelt down and reached out to Malice. Instantly, as his fingers touched Malice, the horse bucked and reared up. Samuel grabbed onto the reins and spoke gently, finally calming the horse down. He felt the bones and muscles of the horse, running his hands over the horses' body, slowly, his fingers searching for anything out of the ordinary. As his fingers made their way along the horses' back, he felt an odd indentation in its muscle. Leaning in closer, he could easily make out a very large, thick scar on its leg. "Maybe he got caught on something," he thought to himself. Feeling around back to its flank, he withdrew his fingers quickly, as if they had been burnt. There were telltale indentations of whip marks along its flank! He turned to look at the other side and saw that there were even worse marks on its other side. It didn't take him long to figure out what had happened. The sheriff was a cruel, cold person, capable of abuse, as he had almost whipped Malice before Samuel shielded him from the blow. But this! When Malevolence was rejected by the sheriff, followed by the whipping, he realized what a cruel, heartless man the sheriff really was. No one deserved to be rejected and whipped. His mind wondered what other kinds of cruelty this animal had known, what other horrible, unspeakable things he had done and seen.

Rage came over Samuel as he whispered to the horse,

A Horse Named Yo-Yo

"I'm sorry, no one deserves this. But you're not good enough to farm with now. You're too damaged, but I realize it's not your fault. I'm sorry for even saying that, but it's true. I gotta keep you, but you're in no shape to tend to what crop I have. I don't even dare give you a name. I can't form a relationship with a tainted animal." He cried softly as he spoke to the animal, hating the words that came from his mouth, but knowing they were true. "I suppose I'll need to find some other use for you."

The day after Yo-Yo was taken; a young man had come to his farm asking for help rounding up his cattle. Samuel was just about to offer his help when he avoided the young man's eyes and quickly bit his tongue, apologizing. After a few months or so of wallowing in his grief, Samuel was at his home, tending to his chores, his injuries nearly healed, when he heard a rough, impatient knock on his door. A familiar looking middle-aged man, dressed in trousers, a wide brimmed straw hat, and a ragged pair of shoes, nearly pounded his door down in urgency.

"Please, Samuel, you have to help me! One of my calves got out of his pen and wandered off… I found him, but he's stuck, and there's a fierce storm a comin'! Please, I'm all alone on my farm. My wife she died years ago, and I'm all he's got left and I…"

Samuel surely knew that no one would ever be this frazzled unless it was a dire emergency. He interrupted, laying his hand on the man's shoulder and reassured him, "It'll be ok. We'll find him, I promise you that. I won't rest until he's safely back home with you." Samuel stood up from his seat, this time not caring about his lack of gear, and almost knocking the chair over, grabbed his coat from the hook on the wall. As he struggled to put it on, flinging the door open, he turned to the stranger, and with hesitation in his voice, asked him where he lived.

"About three miles to the south.... And hurry, those storm clouds don't look none too friendly..." Extending his hand, he added, "By the way, the name's Nathaniel, and I honestly do appreciate this, my friend. I promise to repay you when this is all over."

"No need, my friend. I'm just glad to be able to help."

As they ran, Samuel's mind went back, as it was habit for him to do on occasion, to the day he acquired his new horse. Now, time had passed slowly from when Samuel had won the horse, until now, and try as he might, he just couldn't get this new horse to become friends with him. Though it was a horse, the animal was stubborn as a mule. He diligently tried to train the animal, spending hours with him during the next few days, but to no avail. He felt that working with this horse would be giving false hope that a bond would be formed, and he felt like forming a bond with any other animal, would be almost like giving up on his old friend.

Samuel let out a sigh of both surrender and anger, as the memory of acquiring the new horse passed. Throwing the old saddle on the back of the horse, he vaulted up and over. With a quick glance, he noticed dark, brown storm clouds gathering, the wind kicking up dust so brutal and intense, that he soon wouldn't be able to see his hand in front of his face. With fear in his voice, he and Nathaniel looked at each other, knowing that this was what they feared most. This was a gigantic, terrible storm of dust, instead of rain, that would later come to be known as the Great Dust Bowl.

Samuel knew that they needed to move fast, or there would be no hope for the poor calf. With a loud 'Yahhh', Samuel felt the animal hesitate at first, then stop completely, nearly pitching him forward! This wasn't what he had in mind! He got back on, angrily spurring the horse on again, and felt it charge forward, nearly toppling him off. He hung on with all his strength and felt the land move past him as the horse picked up speed. They were riding along with amazing swiftness, almost too fast. Samuel knew that this horse wanted nothing more than to be with his old master. Even though he was abused, old habits die hard, and all he knew was the sheriff. Shaking his head, he cleared his thoughts and concentrated on the task at hand. He couldn't help but think of that poor defenseless calf out there in the wilderness, totally alone, and his thoughts traveled briefly, to Yo-Yo, and memories of his wife, as he blinked away tears that had come to his eyes.

As time slowly dragged on, they stopped at what seemed to be a large cliff; the blinding dust keeping them from seeing much of anything. Having to guess where they were; they reined in the horses. As they tied their mounts to a couple of scrawny trees, they carefully stepped from their horses and felt their way ahead to the edge of a deep canyon. Struggling to gaze past the storm down into the ravine, they could barely make out the shape of a calf, their eyes quickly filling with grime. After wiping their eyes, and gazing over the canyon a second time, their eyes locked on him once again.

Down near the bottom, they had no idea how far down, a young, brown and white spotted calf lay on his side with his legs spread out at strange angles beneath him. The calf was crying out desperately in pain, as he was trapped between two large boulders. The two men looked at each other, wondering how to rescue this poor creature. The longer they waited, the deeper the dust would become, narrowing their chances for survival.

Nathaniel, nearly beside himself with worry, ran back to his horse, grabbing his rope hanging from the saddle. Using his fingers to find his way along the rope and straighten it out, he tossed one end to Samuel and forced his eyelids open, against the dirt and grime, looking again at the sky. The dust clouds had become thicker and angrier in a matter of minutes. Every second that passed meant that the calf would soon be buried in a sheet of dust, the wind blowing so hard that with every step of progress they made, the dust covered their tracks again, making it impossible for help to come if they needed it. Knowing they had just a short time to make a rescue, Samuel walked carefully up to the edge of the cliff and stepped down softly onto the rock. With each careful footstep, he was increasingly aware of the danger of the situation.

He felt a thick cloud of dust slide down his neck and looked up yet again, grumbling as the storm came in thick waves, making him gasp for air, but every time he did, all he got were thick gravelly mouthfuls of soil. Within a matter of minutes, the penetrating dust had grown even worse. The wind caused the dust to force its way through every nook and cranny, even the noses and mouths of the rescuers. The inability of the rescuers to even breathe properly narrowed the hope for any chance of the poor animal surviving, much less being rescued. Samuel grabbed tight onto the rope, closed his eyes and breathed a silent prayer of protection.

Nathaniel staggered frantically around, as a drunkard, for a sturdy anchor to attach the rope to. Three feet away, on his right stood a tough oak tree, its rough branches turned gray and colorless, barely visible through the tempest. By now, the dust was coming in violent sheets. The ground turned barren and lifeless, being covered completely in a matter of minutes, in a brown, thick dust.

Staggering up to the tree, Nathaniel was careful not to slip and lose his footing. He yelled to Samuel, over the constant howl of the wind, "When I get the rope around the trunk of this tree, I need you to tie the loose end around your waist. Don't do anything else until I tell you to, we could lose this calf, and I can't lose you too!"

He sensed the urgency in Nathaniel's voice and smiled a weak smile, giving him a thumbs-up sign. Samuel could only hope that things really would turn out for the best. Nathaniel walked over to the large tree and embraced it. He began wrapping his rope around it, tugging on it to make sure it held. As soon as he was satisfied, he called over the side to Samuel. Screaming words of encouragement above the storm, he felt proud that he could be able to help his new friend. He began to think of how they would celebrate after this rescue was over, but then remembered that they needed to begin the rescue first. The rope was stretched tight, the dust making it slick, Samuel tested the rope, giving Nathaniel another thumbs up sign. He could see Nathaniel was struggling with tying the rope around him. The rope quickly unraveled from the tree, causing Samuel to run toward the edge of the canyon, "Wait a minute, Nathaniel, the rope loosened a bit, I need to tie it tight again." Samuel yelled to his friend, "Hold tight, we'll get this done, don't move a muscle", tying another, more secure knot, and yelled over the edge, "Now, let's see if we can try this again. It should hold now. I want you to tie the other end around your waist, like I showed you already, keep the knot tight and the rope slack, and when I tell you to, walk very slowly backward, to the edge, but not before I tell you to!"

Nathaniel was shaking as he tied the rope to his waist, wanting to tell Samuel about his worst fear: he was afraid of heights. However, as he looked back at his new friend, the look in Samuel's eyes gave him the courage to keep on going. The dust was pounding at him from every side, so thick that it even blocked out the light of the day. And to think, just an hour or so ago had been completely cloudless! He nervously set his feet on the rock and stepped backward off the cliff, the rope secured tightly around his waist.

Sweat pouring off him, Nathaniel gently lowered himself down into the canyon, one slow step at a time, once nearly losing his footing because of the rough, sharp rocks, barely able to be seen through the dust. Still, as he regained his balance, he became more sure of himself and carefully, but now with more confidence, made his way to the bottom of the canyon. The twenty minutes it took to reach the ground seemed to stretch into days. In the middle of his descent, Nathaniel took a handkerchief from his pocket, with a knot already tied in it, he used one hand to wrap it securely around his mouth so he wouldn't inhale any more dust than he had to, his other hand firmly on the rope. The longer the dust storm went on, the darker it became, the blinding dust choking out what was left of the sun, leaving the sky pitch black.

"You ok down there?" Samuel yelled to Nathaniel, as he slowly made his way down the cliff.

"Yeah, I'm good, just can't see a blasted thing! Just keep letting me down nice and easy."

Samuel thought of closing his eyes to keep from being so scared, but the sky was already pitch black, making it impossible to see anything. Besides, he couldn't close his eyes even if he wanted to, knowing his friend was on the other end of the rope and Samuel had his life in his hands. The thick sheets of dust turned the sky so dark out that even if it was nighttime they wouldn't have even been able to see any stars to light their way, much less the moon. Samuel breathed another prayer of protection, hoping that soon he or Nathaniel would at least hear the calf make any sort of noise, so they would know it was still alive.

Just then, another thought occurred to both men, nearly at the same time. Maybe the reason the calf wasn't making any noise was because of the dust blocking out the sun. If the dust had turned the day into night, then the calf thought his bedtime had arrived. They quickly abandoned that line of thought though, as they foolishly realized that with the position the calf was in, whether it was nighttime or not was probably the least of his worries. Nathaniel adjusted his feet slowly as he descended down the canyon wall. The wind whirled around him, biting his ears, as his left foot found a small ledge. He waited until he felt a little slack in the rope, and then pushed away from the ledge with both feet. At that same instant, the wind seemed to strengthen with intensity, rocking him back and forth.

Nathaniel found himself swaying in the dust filled air, his feet desperately seeking a crevice or ledge that he could use to steady himself. The wind fought back with the force of a heavyweight prizefighter, not giving up, as if it had a personal vendetta against Nathaniel. His frail body slammed mercilessly against the rock wall, once, twice, three times. "God please, if you're out there, help me!" The final blow nearly knocked the breath out of him, sending sharp, jagged splinters of rock gouging into his leg, as the canyon echoed his empty, useless pleas back to him.

Suddenly, out of nowhere, a very faint, high-pitched squeal was heard from the calf! Nathaniel knew he was too far down to warn his friend, so all he was able to do was pray for safety for both him and the calf. He breathed a sigh of relief, but just as suddenly, a frightening thought occurred to him! Even though the calf was alive, the thick dust was still filling in the space between the boulders where he was trapped!

Chapter 4 – March 19, 1930

Nathaniel closed his eyes against the howling wind and dust and felt his way the final few feet, slowly to the bottom of the ravine. Giving a short tug on his rope, he felt it go slack, knowing that Samuel had loosened his hold as soon as he felt the tug. Holding his hands out in front of him like a blind man, Nathaniel put one foot in front of the other as he made his way through the thick dust to where the calf was, the desperate cries of help growing louder.

As Nathaniel's fingers reached out to touch the rocks, he was amazed at the thick layer of dust that had already settled. The dust storm was only a couple hours old and already it seemed there was enough of it to last them a lifetime. Samuel's fingers wrapped around the large rocks, searching for handholds, as the wind battered him, threatening to knock him off balance. The powerful wind made his feet feel like lead, and he grunted with every forced step. Using his last reserves of strength to make it the final few feet, he imagined that this must be where the calf went down, before the storm overtook them, rendering them blind. With one last burdensome step, he nearly lost his balance and went down on one knee. He fully expected his fingers to grasp nothing but air; instead they found the strong, muscular form of a young calf and his fingers embedded tight in its shoulder.

At that moment, the intense wind and blinding soil let up considerably, as if by a miracle; he was now able to know for certain the exact position the calf was lying. Its small, frail body was lodged between two large boulders, each weighing roughly 500 pounds apiece. Nathaniel attempted to move the boulders, but they wouldn't budge. He knew they were too heavy to even consider moving, too much for a normal man to move, for sure. The calf was lodged between the two boulders as its body laid still, its legs bent to one side and its head twisted behind its body. Samuel let out a small groan, afraid that the poor animal was already lost, when he noticed the small rise and fall of its chest.

The animal was still breathing, thank God! Knowing he was too far down to call back up to Samuel, he untied the rope from his waist and wrapped his arm around the animal's neck. Pulling with all his strength, but also as carefully as he could manage, he finally was able to free the calf's head. The calf turned around to look in his eyes, and he was amazed at how this animal had managed to survive under these conditions for this long. Putting his hand under the calf's body, he managed to wriggle the animal free of its prison, very slowly dragging him to safety. Taking off his jacket, he wrapped it around the animal's nose and mouth firmly, but loose enough that it was still able to breathe. He needed to keep the calf's airway free, so he wouldn't suffocate on the blowing dust, would it decide to kick back up again.

Making his way down into the shallow, rocky valley between the two boulders and behind where the calf was stuck, Nathaniel felt his way among the smooth rocks, until he came to a place where a few of the rocks were missing. Out of this area, a cool, gentle draft of air flowed. Samuel knelt down slowly and pressed his face to it, as a cool, refreshing breeze flowed over his face. He was guessing that this must have been the place where the calf had his mouth, as the edges of the vent were thick with saliva. His head would have to have been twisted at just the right angle so this fresh current of air could shield him from the chaos around him and protect him from harm, at the same time giving him much needed air to keep him alive. With his strong hands under the calf, supporting him, he slowly dragged the poor animal to safety, in the recess of the face of the cliff, using his own body to shield the poor animal from the elements.

With several long tugs of the thick, dirt encrusted rope, the howling wind and grime causing them to nearly lose their grip many times, Samuel nearly pulled the poor calf up to almost the edge of the cliff. His breath came in short gasps and his body shook from the exertion as the dust clung to his sweaty frame, he called over to Nathaniel, the cries of the calf barely audible through the storm. Nathaniel tried answering with a cry of desperation as he realized they were close to the end of their rescue, but it wasn't finished until everyone was safe. Samuel heard his cries as the wind carried them, and very gradually made his way the final short distance to the edge of the cliff, making sure not to look down, so as not to lose his concentration. He thought briefly of yelling to his buddy that he had almost made it, when he thought of a better idea.

There, in a small fissure in the rock, immediately to his right, lay a worn tin can, with a torn label still readable on it. Taking the rope tightly in his hands as his muscles protested and strained against his every move, he pulled the end of the rope over to a strong boulder, which was roughly ten feet high and weighing many tons. This particular boulder being large enough to support a very large amount of weight, such as this poor animal, he slowly made his way around the rock, tying the rope around its diameter.

When he was satisfied that the knot was tight enough and wouldn't come undone, as he remembered his father teaching him to do at home years ago, he gave it one last quick yank. Crawling on his knees now, the force of the strong wind too much for him to stay upright, he felt along the stony ground for the tin can. Finally wrapping his hands around it, Samuel used his other hand and fished around in his pockets for what he was looking for.

As Samuel tilted his face upwards and closed his eyes, he breathed a short prayer of thankfulness to God and attempted to get the calf ready to be pulled up the cliff and taken back to relative safety. Grabbing the calf delicately, they tied the rope securely around the calf and Samuel pulled him up to safety. Every so often, during his task, he stared over at the boulder and turned his head to look at the calf, taking turns doing so, making sure that neither of them was going anywhere. He had to admit, in the middle of this mess, watching this poor animal suspending many feet above a deep canyon, with the rope wrapped around his belly, just dangling there, was quite a comical sight, one that made him chuckle in the midst of all this literally swirling chaos. Nathaniel hoisted himself up the final few feet, and just lay there, panting in exhaustion.

Picking himself up after his brief rest, his fingers fumbling around in his pockets a second time, a silent plea of help escaping his parched, cracked lips, his fingers finally sliding along the edge of what he had been searching for all along. Samuel let out a small cry of pain as his pointer finger pricked the edge of a small knife. Ignoring the point of blood bubbling to the surface of his finger, he withdrew the sharp object and, placing the tin can firmly against the ground, he wrapped the scarf again

A Horse Named Yo-Yo

around his face, as tight as he could make it, without cutting off his air. With the wind whipping mercilessly around him, he raised the blade of the knife to the tin can, when he heard a peculiar sound. In the distance, a very faint humming noise could be heard.

After a few minutes, the humming sound grew steadily to a loud chirp. In all the chaos and confusion, neither Samuel nor Nathaniel had noticed that the wind had died down greatly, which also caused the dust storm to weaken and eventually disappear as well. Breathing a deep sigh of relief, Nathaniel brought the point of the knife sharply against the bottom of the tin can, a few sharp thrusts making a small hole in the bottom.

As the chirping sound grew louder gradually, he muttered to himself, "What is that racket?" Staring up into the distance, he glimpsed a terrible sight, as his eyes grew wide, and his mouth hung open slack jawed. This was the worst thing any farmer wanted to see, and something that would haunt him for many years to come! Nathaniel screamed to his partner, hoping the wind would carry his words, "They won't harm anything, there's no crop here for them to destroy." Forgetting about the tin can, he threw it down, sending it tumbling over the edge. There were more important things to worry about now. Nathaniel screamed again, and then paused a minute. Soon he heard the voice of Samuel saying, I hear you, I'm coming down!" As Samuel soon made his way to where Nathaniel was, they quickly got back on their horses, the calf awkwardly positioned between them, their horses flying from out of the canyon as fast as possible!

When they got back to the truck, Samuel and Nathaniel gently laid him in the bed of the truck and quickly got in. They started up the vehicle and made their way down the dirt road. "There's a vet not too far away. We can take him there. He'll be all right, promise." Samuel said. Nathaniel didn't look convinced but he was too weary to argue the matter. Samuel added, "When he's better, I'll get him back to you safe and sound, I promise." As they drove along, with Nathaniel at the wheel, Samuel closed his eyes and breathed the cool night air, thankful that the storm had passed. Still, a heavy haze persisted as the remainder of the dust settled to the ground. He looked up into the sky and smiled.

What he saw next caused him to stare slack jawed into the night sky, though. Looking up at the stars, he could barely make out the constellations through the oppressive haze. As the stars brightened though, they seemed to form a specific pattern. It seemed a message had suddenly and mysteriously materialized! The stars had begun to form letters, pinpoints of light where everything else was total darkness. Order appeared in the midst of randomness. To anyone else, it wouldn't make sense, but to him, it was plain as the nose on his face. Someone was looking out for them after all, and had a message created and written just for him: '*Hope is a flame.*' Samuel read the divine message slowly, twinkling among the vastness of space. He carefully rubbed his chin, pondering the meaning of it all.

Chapter 5: March 21, 1930

    As the lonely cart slowly trudged past broken farmhouses and old forgotten fields, Yo-Yo had no choice but to breathe a long, drawn out sigh, his mood darkening with every beat of his tiny heart. With the cart trudging its way wearily across the dusty old road, he gazed out to the clouds, again trying to imagine shapes in them. But it was no use, now all they looked like were just lonely old clouds. As they made their way past a farm he was raised in for a while, his mind wandered to the event of his birth and his family. Once, long ago, they had a peaceful, carefree existence that no one could interrupt.
    He was told, by various friends of Samuel, that in the late 1800's, he was born in the beautiful state of Minnesota, the son of a whitish-gray stallion named Cyrus and a brown and white speckled mare named Hannah. His father was a wild horse who could always be seen wildly racing against the other horses in the field as to who was the fastest. Usually his father won, but occasionally he was given a lesson in humility, which is good for anyone to learn occasionally.
    As the Great Depression loomed, Yo-Yo remembered one particular sunny day, their owner, a strong young man with a handsome face and a fairly thick goatee named Trace, and his two hired hands, a couple of middle aged men named Grant and Kyler, walked out to the field to give them a special treat of hay and grain. The pasture, that they spent a good amount of time in, was situated close enough to the house that, he could peer over the fence and see the glow from the small TV that their owners were watching. They were fortunate and blessed,

as it was one of the very few in the nation at that time. They also listened to dramatic programs on the radio. Grant peered into the window, carrying the buckets of grain, to see his friend Trace's younger siblings, two sweet, young girls named Payton and Lexi, eagerly watch Snow White and the Seven Dwarfs on TV. The adults gathered in the room next to them, listening to the upbeat sounds of jazz musician, Duke Ellington.

The next day, the two girls went outside to the pasture, to brush Cyrus' mane. A favorite pastime involved reciting stories as they worked, to help pass the time. Today, it was The Three Little Pigs, tomorrow, who knows. Their parents were grateful for the chance to get them out of the house, as well as to have cheap activities to keep them busy in these rough times.

On this specific day, joyful, uplifting voices wafted from the house. The owners of the homestead, a young and very much in love couple named Thomas and Sarah, had brought company over to play cards. Thomas was soberly telling the couple of his adventures, long ago, during the war. He was a soldier during World War I, and would regularly get letters from this girl that he had come to know, before the war. Months passed, and in one particular letter, he wrote of how they dreamed of having a horse one day. At the end of the letter, he professed his love to her and proposed. No sooner had he written the letter, he said, than a horse appeared out of nowhere, and knelt down, licking the top of his head. He thought nothing of the incident, and days later, he mailed the letter off, along with his grandfather's ring, requesting her hand in marriage. Well, after he had mailed that letter, he saw that horse arriving as a sign, and decided to call the horse Cyrus. Then he proudly pointed to a horse in the distance, grazing on a pile of hay.

He then told them, as they finished the card game, that as soon as he met Cyrus, it was like something came over him, and he knew what he had to do. "Why, I made my way outta that trench", he said, "and I got up on Cyrus' back, and I turned the horse around. Cyrus and I, we made our way a short distance, when I saw an old cavalry sword hidden in some bushes. I picked it up, said a prayer for the fallen soldier, as is the right and proper thing to do, and we made our way down a hill into the thick of the fighting. There was times I thought we'd never get outta there, alive or dead. But the Good Lord always saw fit to provide and keep us safe. The men in my care, they were in that trench talking among themselves and wondering what was happening, when me and Cyrus left. Honestly, I wondering what was happening too. Something musta come over 'em though, cause me and ol' Cyrus, hadn't traveled more than a mile, and I heard whoops and shouts behind me. Well, I turned my head and smiled wider than you ever seen! Every single one of my men was following me, weapons at the ready. Suppose the Good Lord knew I couldn't go it alone, so He gave me help when I needed it."

"I remember one particular day, it was cold and raining. Well, my bunkmate had along a radio. Good thing too, cause we was about to go crazy, if all we had to listen to were that gunfire all around us! Anyways, it was during fall, the start of football season. He turned it on and, I tell ya what! We heard the biggest crowd you ever did hear in your life! The announcer was goin' on about this new group of young men, just begun playin' competitively in 1890, they did. Well, he was talkin 'bout how they were all dirt poor, but real hard workers. A tough team they were! Called themselves the Bugeaters at first; strange name, I thought, but I s'ppose it made sense later. That squad, they're a good bunch they are. Some of 'em, the ones who were reserves, was soldiers in my troop, so I was fortunate enough to meet em. Got some autographs, I did. Anyways, forgive me; I'm getting off track a bit. Cyrus and I, well, we met face to face that day, and well, later on, he became Yo-Yo's father. God bless that poor horse! Must be scared to death! Hope everyone involved finds what they come looking for. Yeah, after I proposed to Sarah, we were married when I come home. It was nothing but a simple ceremony, nothing fancy. She always said, long as she had me, everything else was just a detail," he said blushing deeply. At that moment, Sarah came over, laying a hand on his strong shoulder.

Thomas continued speaking as the company listened intently, "When we were married", at this, Sarah wrapped her arm around him, nestling against his side, "we built us this here house, and we had many a memory in it. Had us a son, he went off to play baseball. We followed the game as best we could, we did. We quickly became a fan of the Yankees, followin' the likes of Babe Ruth and Joe Dimaggio. Both of 'em played for the Yankees, different times of course. We was glad our son got the opportunity to play with 'em."

Thomas had just barely finished his story, when the candles suddenly flickered on and off, the wind picking up violently. "It's ok, just another dust storm, had a lot of em lately. They just pick up and just as sudden, they're over." Thomas calmly replied. Sarah was more careful and alert than he was, though. She tore away from his side and ran to close all the windows, plugging up as many holes as could be blocked. Thomas threw down his cards

A Horse Named Yo-Yo

and said impatiently, "Well, I suppose we gotta get down there and safe. Let's go!" They led the company into the cellar, and soon they were huddling around the only radio. As the whistle of the relentless wind swept through, Thomas and Sarah made their way into the cellar soon after the rest of the people. "We gotta get the children!" Sarah screamed in horror! "They'll be fine", Thomas reassured her. "Trace knows to take 'em the back way into the cellar! He'd never let anything happen to 'em!" They'll be there, you'll see!"

Sarah made her way down into the cellar, anxiously, as she was greeted in hushed voices, by the other visitors. Minutes had passed, as they held hands, praying the storm would soon pass. Quietly, Thomas reached over and turned on the radio, as he had done many times before. As they listened to the songs coming over the radio, a calming voice interrupted, speaking the Good News of Jesus Christ. The company listened, and in the midst of uncertainty and fear, many in that cellar that night abandoned their fear, and accepted Christ as their Savior. As soon as they had finished, a loud knock echoed through the cellar as the door swung open! Covered in dust from head to toe, their mouths and noses covered with rags, Trace, Grant, Kyler, Payton, and Lexi, all stepped into the darkness of the cellar, and immediately, they were wrapped in hugs as tears streamed down the faces of their loved ones. "We thought we'd lost you for good... Don't be ever doin' nothing like that again!" one of the men scolded. Noah quickly said, "It's ok, they were lost and now they're found, and so are we." The children wondered what Noah meant but they were just glad to be safe and sound. They all gathered around the small radio and said a prayer for each other, as they held one another close. As the prayer ended, Thomas and Sarah told their children what they had meant by "being found", and as they were simply told the truth of God's love, each one of the children gave their lives to their Heavenly Father.

Nearly an hour passed, as the storm finally died down, late into the night. Everyone carefully made their way up the steps and opened the door. Barely able to see through the darkness, Sarah and Thomas looked down as a large rabbit hopped into their house! Sarah quickly got a broom and swung hard at the animal! "Shoo, get outta here!" she said. Turning to the company, she warned, "Can't have any more comin' in. We'd best sleep in the cellar tonight." She handed Trace a rifle, "Here, if any get through, take care of 'em. I'm against shootin' innocent animals, but they come and invaded our land. They can't eat what we got planted for food, we won't allow it! That field's all we got. We lose it, not sure what we'll do. So take care of 'em if they do come this way. Besides, we need food, rabbits make good meat." Trace took the gun and sat against a chair. The rest of them made their way back to the cellar and slept rather comfortably, the rest of the night passing uneventfully. Early in the morning, Sarah and Thomas opened their eyes and stretching, walked up the stairs, and opened the door of the cellar. Thomas placed his hand on the door leading outside and turned the knob. Placing his hand on his mother's wrist, Trace spoke up urgently, "I'm sorry, there was just too many of em... I tried..." Thomas' eyes became wide as saucers as he opened the door wide, a low helpless moan escaped his lips. In his grief, he whispered, It's ok, Trace. It ain't your fault." Bringing his shaking fingers to his lips, tears fell from Thomas' face. Where once stood his field, only a barren landscape now lay. In its place stood nothing more than a square patch of useless dirt, now completely covered with layers upon layers of rabbits! The moving, writhing mass of thousands of the animals quickly destroying everything that was left!

Sarah came running behind and when she saw what had happened, she pulled up short, tears streaming down her face, as she buried her head in Thomas' chest. "What shall we do now!" she cried. "That was all we had! We got nothing left!" The rest of the company came to see what the commotion was, and when they saw the devastation, they simply embraced Thomas and Sarah, whispering empty words of comfort. Thomas and Sarah fell to their knees as the realization of what had been done came crashing down on them like a furious wind. They knew know that there was nothing left for them here. They would be forced to move, far from all their friends and family, and their once certain future was now uncertain.

As their friends cried helplessly for Thomas and Sarah, and all they had to go through, a small, frail boy on crutches came forth, and jostling his way toward them, began to speak in a soft, yet powerful voice. He stammered, but in his own innocent way, reminded them that were surrounded by a group of believers now, and God would use this for good. His blessings would be shown through tears, and His joy would come in the morning. Thomas and Sarah managed weak smiles as they were reminded once again that no matter what came their way, with friends who were willing to lift them up and stand by them, and with God on their side, nothing could stand against them. Embraced by their friends, Noah and Sarah stood up and resolutely looked upon their livelihood, now gone. The young children stood a short distance off, holding hands, as they prayed earnestly for a miracle. With tears in their eyes, parents and children alike vowed that they would help rebuild, somehow. This was an enormous disappointment, to say the very least. Some of their friends had the same thing happen, only to break under the strain of it. But with their friends and family surrounding them, one thing was certain in that moment. With God on their side, they may bend by the winds of change, but they would never, ever break.

A Horse Named Yo-Yo

Chapter 6: May 1, 1930

As the small cart trudged along, carrying its precious cargo, Yo-Yo hung his head sadly, as his mind was yanked sharply back to reality. True, life was different than it had been, but maybe, just maybe, there were lessons to be learned that could help them on their journey. As he thought about this, the wagon jerked suddenly and he heard the few men at the front of the wagon yell to each other angrily, but everything was a jumble of voices and no words could be understood properly. Suddenly, within a couple of minutes, a large thick tarp was pulled over the wagon that was being hauled by the pickup truck, completely covering everything and making it nearly impossible to see.

Yo-yo felt a hand snake through the tarp and yank hard on his bridle, bringing him to his knees in obedience. His breathing quickening as he was faced with something else he didn't understand yet, like all the other things he had faced so far. A thick, deep voice silenced him as he lowered his head, pricked up his ears and listened, the voice falling quiet as quickly as it had come.

Nothing but silence could be heard all around. Not even the voices of the men, who had just a moment ago been running around, were heard. Yo-Yo wondered where they had gone to, when his ears pricked up again. Something was happening! At first, it sounded like the gentle buzz of an automobile engine. But, within a matter of minutes, the steady hum of whatever was coming got louder and louder, until it was so loud that Yo-Yo could not even hear himself think, and for that to happen, noises had to be very loud. As the noise increased, so did his

Kyle Nathan Buller

confusion.

He wondered what was causing this racket, but he also knew the men wouldn't have covered the trailer and pickup this tightly without a very good reason. He may have no idea where they were headed, and what would happen to him when he got there, but he knew that these men were just doing what they were told to do, they really didn't mean him any harm.

Yo-Yo stood up slowly on his legs and backed away quietly from the tarp, the small size of the wagon not giving him much room to move. His eyes darting from right to left and back again, looking for movement on the light tan sheet, anything that would tell him what was going on. After a minute or so of searching, his eyes landed on a light green shape among the tarp, the darker shade of green standing out against the tarp.

Slowly moving forward on his legs, his face came closer to the shape. A large, light green bug with legs and antennae was crawling slowly up the tarp. At first, he was confused but then remembered what it was. When he was just a young foal, years ago, during the races with his father, his mother anxiously looking on, he would sometimes win the race, only to have these same types of bugs crawl across his face, and he would have to shake his mane to get them off. He later learned they were known as grasshoppers. However, little did he know the swarming mass of hundreds of thousands that awaited them on the other side of this blanket.

One of the men screamed and cursed at the insects as they slid across his body, his arms flailing as his shadow moved across the tarp. As the man continued to flail his arms, he was about to throw back the tarp to unleash the insects inside. Instead he carefully knelt down, stuffing the remaining ends of the tarp securely inside the wagon, forming a seal that the grasshoppers could not get through. At the instant he formed the seal; he knelt down quickly as his arms flailed against the onslaught. Soon, his body thrashed violently around on the ground in an attempt to get the bugs off.

Yo-Yo looked up and, with the horrible buzzing sound filling his ears and threatening to drive him crazy, he stared quietly at the tarp. Where the light tan color of the tarp was just a short time ago, it had now changed to a pitch black, the gigantic number of insects feeding off the material, as an angry buzz grew to not only the one side of the trailer, but now surrounding him. The other side of the tarp was literally crawling with thousands of grasshoppers. He whimpered softly as he knelt down again, breathed a defeated sigh, realizing they were trapped!

Chapter 7: May 2, 1930

The next day, as the early morning sun's rays broke through the sky, Samuel drove over to Nathaniel's place and picked him up. Nathaniel excitedly got in his pickup truck and they made their way over to the vet, where the calf was being cared for. The entire way, Nathaniel kept talking about how excited he was to finally see his calf again. "Tell you what, he better be feeling great, long as it took for us to find him. We went to a lot of trouble to rescue the poor thing." Samuel just nodded, though he knew if the good Lord hadn't protected them, the calf would have surely died. It took roughly 15 minutes, over a rough, dusty trail, to reach their destination. As they slowly got out of his truck, they were greeted by the vet, a sweet lady, with golden curls falling over her shoulders, named Madison. She reached out her hand to shake Samuel's firmly, then turned to shake Nathaniel's hand as well. "Hello Samuel, hello, Nathaniel. My name is Madison. Your friend's calf is doing just fine. He was scared when you brought him in, but he's recovered nicely, he's a real fighter."

As she was talking, a young lady, just barely out of her teen years, looked up at Samuel and smiled innocently. Holding her fingers to her forehead, Madison said, "I don't know what the matter with me is today. I've been forgetting all sorts of things. This here is my assistant, Erica. We've been working hard to bring him back to full health. We've come across cases like this one before. Usually calves that are brought in like this, have too much dust in their lungs and they die soon. But someone must have been making real sure he was protected. He hasn't suffered any broken bones from what I can see, and the sounds he's making, are normal. I can't tell much dust has entered his lungs, not enough that it'll do any lasting damage, at least. Samuel said to Madison and Erica, "Maybe we should leave him here a couple more days, just so we know he's gonna pull through ok.. "No, it's fine, we'll take him home now", Nathaniel very quickly interrupted. Samuel looked over at his friend's pleading eyes and let out a sigh, "Ok, he's gonna take him home now, I believe." Instantly, the sides of Nathaniel's mouth turned up and he grinned wider than he ever had.

After they had paid the vet, Samuel and Nathaniel shook hands with Madison and her assistant and got up to leave. As they opened the door, Nathaniel looked back at the ladies and smiled. His face turned a deep shade of red. Madison and Erica looked on, playing with the hair, as they stared back at him. The calf was being led on a leash as they made their way to the truck. As Nathaniel took a step down, his feet slipped on a pile of dog dung. At the same instant, they flew out from under him, causing him to land face first in a large pile of pig slop. Nathaniel just lay there for a minute, either from pain or pure embarrassment. The episode must have spooked the poor calf, because, before he knew it, the leash had wrapped around Nathaniel's legs! The calf was running straight ahead, as fast as he could, dragging poor Nathaniel behind him!

His body bounced off the road as he was hauled a few yards, then just as suddenly, the calf stopped. Nathaniel's momentum caused him to slide forward, then just as suddenly he stopped. Nathaniel struggled to sit up, his head throbbing. Before he had time to react, he was met by the calf, as it rudely sat atop Nathaniel's face!

Placing his hands around the torso of the animal, he lifted him up slowly and set the calf aside. As he spit out globs of slop from his mouth, a young pig came up and licked him on the face, washing off the mess. As Nathaniel lifted himself up from the grime, Samuel quickly ran over and held out a hand to lift him up, but he angrily shrugged it off, saying gruffly, "I can do it myself, thank you very much!" Erica and Madison followed behind him closely, running to help poor Nathaniel as well, which only succeeded in making him more embarrassed and upset. As he got to his feet, Nathaniel looked down to see he was covered head to toe in a sloppy, dusty mess. He had unfortunately lost his hat as well. He lifted his head meekly to see the two women standing before him, their hands covering their mouth and noses, more from the stench than anything else. Running his hand through his hair, he lowered his head, bowing in respect, "Thank you ladies." As he said this, he coughed and sputtered, spitting out thick globs of mud. The ladies' eyes widened as they looked at each other and giggled, very much amused.

    They laughed silently as Nathaniel placed his hand on the door of the truck, yanking it open! To make things worse, at the same instant he opened the door, out of nowhere, a sudden gust of wind caught his hand, and it slipped on the handle, hitting him square on his nose. The collision caused him to crumple down on the ground! Groaning in pain, Nathaniel held his nose, now bleeding, and finally managed to make it into the truck. As Nathaniel held a rag to his aching nose, Samuel went around back and prodded the calf into the back of the truck, laughing to himself silently all the while. Slamming the bed of the truck, Samuel walked around to the other side, opened the door and got in. Placing his hands on the steering wheel, he paused just a minute, a wide smile forming on his face. Nathaniel whispered gruffly, his nose in the air, the rag quickly turning blood red, "Just drive, Samuel! I gotta get home and get cleaned up!"

"Whatever you say, y'know, you really don't have to be in such a bad mood. You were a hit with the ladies back there." Samuel said, Nathaniel's icy glare bore through him, as Samuel smiled back goofily. In silence, they made their way back to Nathaniel's place, though Samuel tried to cheer him up as best he could. As he pulled into his friend's home, Samuel opened the gate of the truck and herded the calf safely back into his pen, as Nathaniel went inside to get cleaned up. As soon as he was safely in his pen, Samuel got back in his truck, making his way off the property. On the slow drive home, Samuel laughed aloud, as he imagined that he could almost hear the calf himself laughing in amusement.

Chapter 8: The evening of May 3, 1930

As the men driving the truck, with Yo-Yo in tow, scampered quickly around the wagon in an attempt to get rid of this new, horrible plague, Yo-Yo realized that, as he wasn't going anywhere anytime soon, he should probably make the best of his situation and find something to eat. Staring at the grasshopper on the tarp, he leaned his head down and quietly chewed on the mound of hay in the center of the wagon. After a little while of chewing contentedly on his hay, he looked up, startled, his eyes growing wider as he gazed around the large wagon. There, in the corner, a flash of movement caught his eye! At first, it was only a small rustle as the straw and hay moved around, but grew quickly as a thin black shape stood up from the bottom of the wagon.

Yo-Yo's eyes widened and he drew back in fear, his legs shaking as he shrank back to the far corner of the wagon. A loud whinny escaped his mouth as he shook his head in fright, the menacing figure growing larger every second. It grew from an unknown shape and finally formed into the shape of a man. This man was very old, as Yo-Yo noticed by looking into his eyes, his wizened but wrinkled face betraying his years. This particular man was obviously a farmer from one of the nearby towns, as he had dirty overalls on and an old worn straw hat stood on his head.

As he stood up on weak legs, pieces of straw clung thickly to his frail frame, blending with his straw hat, causing him to look like some sort of angry hay monster. Yo-Yo's eyes traveled carefully down the stranger, his curiosity growing as his breathing slowed. Past the bony face, with the sunken eyes, a pair of overalls hung loosely on him, a long, thick, scraggly beard hanging from his face as well, and the end of it nearly touching the bottom of the wagon.

With a series of slow, methodical movements, the mysterious man brought out from behind him a thick staff of wood, apparently his walking stick. He ever so slowly brought it in front of him and tapped it on the ground three times, the whole task seeming to take many minutes. This caused Yo-Yo to buckle his legs beneath him, as he once again collapsed to the ground slowly. Staring up at the stranger in curiosity but also in fearful respect, he lowered his eyes a minute later, as the stranger spoke in a soft, gravelly voice, but one that also commanded reverence.

"You don't know who I am, my friend, but I know you all too well. I have been watching you for a long time now, and I know that you have been handed some things in your short life that you would rather not face. I also know that you are afraid, the darkness is a scary place, much like the darkness as these grasshoppers and dust clouds have covered the sky, drowning out the sunlight. Your master has left you out here in this big world, you are letting yourself be led to places that you have never seen before, but I have been sent here to you with an important message. I want you to take it with you through the rest of your journey. Listen carefully, my friend. Your master and companion has never abandoned you. When you were sold, his heart was breaking just as yours was."

"One of the last things he uttered was a silent prayer that he would somehow be able to see you again. I am here to answer that request, but it may not be in the way you expect. My master does things differently than you may expect, but He does them with love, always with kindness and compassion. Take heart, you will see your master again, possibly sooner than either of you expect. Every night since you two were separated has been filled with prayers on your behalf. I know it may seem right now that you have been on your own this far, but you have not. Forces you aren't even aware of have been struggling and fighting on your behalf, against obstacles that are thrown in your way by the Enemy. Yes, there are more trials to come, but I want you to know that you will come through them safe. Through these trials, there are lessons that you must be prepared to learn. But you are loved much more than you know."

'What are these lessons I need to learn,' Yo-Yo thought to himself.

As if in response, the stranger spoke again. "If I told you all of the answers, it wouldn't be near as exciting to learn those lessons. Years from now, people will believe that life is about the journey, and not the destination. However, you must listen to that still small voice you hear swirling around the confusion, because although the journey is sweet and sometimes bitter as well, it is the destination that makes all the difference. The journey along the way merely gives us patience, courage and determination to reach our goal, as He places people in our path, to show us the way."

"What way is that?" Yo-Yo asked himself, deep in thought.

"I think you already know the answer", the old man whispered.

Throughout their conversation, Yo-Yo noticed that the grasshoppers were finding their way into the wagon in swarms. Soon the thick masses swarmed and crawled over each other as they fought their way against Yo-Yo. Strangely calmed by the words of the mysterious stranger, Yo-Yo stood his ground as thick masses of the insects rushed up against him. Eventually, he had to lie down against the hay and scratch his body against the thick straw to relieve his body against the relentless swarm. As he was rolling around in search of relief, shouts came from the front of the wagon; Yo-Yo recognized them as the men driving the wagons.

He heard footsteps as they drew closer to the wagon. Then suddenly a thick hand pulled open the door violently as one of the men jumped in. His brown eyes wide in terror, he whipped his head back and forth around the wagon, as if searching for something. There, lying in a crate in the corner, he finally found what he had been searching for. In several short strides he reached a thick wooden crate. Prying his fingers firmly between the crate and the edge of the lid, he pulled the top off the crate and wrenched out its contents!

Chapter 9: March 16, 1900

Victorian England: nearly 30 years earlier... A young man in a well pressed brown suit and a bowler hat, stared intently out the window of his high rise apartment, his fingers absentmindedly reaching up to twiddle his mustache, his eyes scanning the street from right to left. As he scans the windows of the buildings, his gaze is drawn upward to birds flying freely, among the clouds, finally falling on what he had been searching for all this time. A middle aged, blonde haired woman in a blue silk dress stepped gingerly off a stagecoach, her dirty blonde hair, lightly tinted by gray, falling around her shoulders. The young man smiled softly as his eyes turned aside, nodding to a shadowy form in the corner of the room. Beside the figure, a fireplace was burning logs, giving the stranger a mysterious glow, as he extended his cane and got to his feet.

"Has the woman arrived?" Alex softly whispered. "Yes, she is coming our way as we speak." The younger man sighed in anticipation, yet his voice quivered with uncertainty. Alex spoke next, a hint of superiority in his voice, "I'm sorry, this is what must be done. It is out of our hands now. We have tried other ways, but this is now the only path we have left." "But, are you sure there isn't another way?" the young man asked.

"Yes, I am sure", Alex spoke, with finality, as he limped over to the other fellow. "This lady should be here very soon", he said, pulling his pocket watch out, "and she has something I want, something I lost long ago." "Maybe it's in one of her pockets, in which case, she could have lost it already...." the younger man desperately hoped, although he knew what his friend was really searching for couldn't be found in any pocket, the reality of it all causing the man to tremble.

"But you do realize she just got married!" the younger man added desperately.

"Yes… I know that, and this man whom she is so "in love" with, will have something terrible revealed to him, something that just may break his faith and his spirit and leave him without what I lost long ago… hope." With these words, he pointed his cane at the younger man.

"And you…."he bellowed, "Will be the one to give her the news. His body shook as he uttered his next words,

"And if I don't?" he replied defiantly.

"Surely you remember your job. Years ago you may remember that you were elected unanimously as the mayor of this town", he hissed, "…you wouldn't want that to come…crashing down… around you, because of a newspaper article, revealing all your "business practices"… now would you?"

"You wouldn't!" the younger man dared, staring defiantly into the eyes of this evil man.

"I suggest you do what I ask, if you don't want to know the answer to that question", Alex answered coldly.

"How could you be so cruel? I'm sure you weren't always like this… What has happened to you?"

"I'll gladly share my story with you both, just as soon as our friend arrives….Trust me… she will want to hear this as well", his voice softening as the flames from the fireplace danced across his features, sending a chill along the younger man's back, even though the room was very warm. After a few tense minutes, a scuffle, followed by uneven footsteps could be heard, as woman's voice got louder and closer.

"The police will hear about this!" the woman cried, as the door opened roughly, and she was shoved through the opening, landing on all fours, as pain shot up through her arm.

"Well, she's here...finally..." Alex smiled wide, in twisted delight. "Shall we get started?"

Turning sharply to the woman, he whispered close to her ear, "You may have a seat...Taylor..." as a pair of large hands roughly pushed her to a large ornate wooden chair in the center of the room. "It's only right that you get the center of the room... after all... you are the guest... of... honor..."

Alex took off his bowler hat, and placed it on the floor, sitting down on a chair slowly, his fingers under his chin as he stared thoughtfully, rubbing his goatee, as if looking into the past for answers. Finally, his deep voice broke the silence. "I am afraid I must give you the shortened version... I have an appointment I must attend to". As his eyes locked on Taylor's, she quickly turned her eyes away from his to the floor, careful not to look at him, but she felt the chill in the room nevertheless.

Chapter 10: Middle of the night on March 16, 1900

"It was a cold, stormy night, when I was born to my parents, a couple of traveling preachers from Oklahoma. I remember many times as a young boy, I was taken to their services and, yes, it did have an effect on me." At this, Alex got up slowly from his chair, walked over to the corner of the room, his cane tapping loudly on the wooden floor, as he poured himself a drink from an ornate pitcher sitting on a bench. Turning back to them abruptly, he took a sip and set the glass down again. "I remember my parents would set up this tent, every night, a large red one with plenty of room for the whole town, it seemed. I would stay silent during the services on a wooden bench. I wanted to see my parents…" he paused, as he thought of his family. My heart swelled with pride as I watched them walk out on stage."

"I remember one still, cold night in particular. We had just finished up one of our services, it was a long trip… traveled halfway across the country, to let these people listen to us. Like I said, we were traveling preachers; we gave the Good News to anyone who would listen. Many nights our tents were filled to overflowing. Sometimes I feared our tent would come crashing down from all the people inside. Most of them just stood, because there weren't enough benches to hold 'em all…. Anyway, as I said, we had just finished up one of our better services and were cleaning up for the night….when, through the opening flap of the tent; I heard a loud howl, from a wolf or some animal of that sort. I picked up my lantern slowly and walked softly over to the opening, my feet careful not to make any noise in the grass. I couldn't afford to disturb whatever had made the noise; I didn't have even a stick to defend myself with whatever lay on the other side of that tent. As I stretched out my arm to extend my lantern, I peered into the darkness, and placing my fingers against the tent flap, I moved it aside very gently."

"A sudden gust of wind ruffled my hair as I opened the tent, my head whipping to the other side against the sharp breeze. Out of the corner of my eye, I saw movement, as a figure in the distance turned the corner into an alley. The moonlight illuminated the shapes in the alleyway, as I carefully made my way down the street to get a closer look. Another figure seemed to be running close behind. in the same direction. I pulled up, barely able to move, as something about the figure became familiar to me. I never did get a look at his face, it was more what he was wearing. He had on a torn white shirt that was caked with mud. As cold fear snaked down my neck, I ran for my life, going as fast as my little legs would carry me." Through gritted teeth, Alex clenched his fists as he looked forward, his eyes never wavering from the window, "I know what I saw, Taylor. That shirt he had on, I saw a man wearing that same shirt many times. Your precious Samuel... the shirt belonged to him. I know it was him! There is no doubt! He was in the same place as me, he worked with me in the tent, why would he not be there?" Taylor screamed, NO! It's not true!" Alex glared at her, his eyes deep and dark, "I know what I saw, and nothing you can say convinces me otherwise." He let out a deep breath and sat back down again slowly, tears running down his cheeks as he began the conclusion of his story, barely speaking above a whisper, as if the end of his tale was almost too sad to tell. With tears warming his cheeks, he continued his miserable account, "I pulled up sharply and….turned the corner… the sound I had heard wasn't any animal. My father sat a few feet away from me, his back against the brick wall as his body shook with sobs. Walking up to him slowly, I reached out my hand and…" at this point, Alex could barely go on, his own body shaking gently with his own sobs as he remembered what had happened. Even though Taylor was a prisoner in this man's house, she felt like rushing over, to at least put her hand on his shoulder, but the fact she was a prisoner prevented her from doing so.

He slowly continued, "I reached out to my father's shoulder and he flinched, but slowly pressed his body to the wall, so I could see what had happened. He figured that I had entered adulthood; I might as well be able to deal with whatever it brought. As he backed up to the wall, I briefly saw a terrible sight! A wail escaped my lips and I tried desperately to claw my way to her, but he held me back... My poor mother was slumped over in the alley, her dress stained with mud… and…" Alex pressed his face to his hands and wiped away thick tears as he continued…"I don't remember anything else really, at that moment; a large hand pressed me to its chest, as my father held me, crying wordlessly. I tried to tear away and get one last look, but again he pressed me to his chest, saying as the tears poured down his cheeks, 'You don't need to see that…..she was so young……Remember her as she was…….he was just a thief…she was…just...in the wrong place…at the wrong time…'

"I remember collapsing in my father's arms, as he held me for the longest time. Then I remember falling asleep, I must have been out for a while. When I awoke, I don't remember feeling anything. All I can remember is a large hole in the pit of my stomach and standing up on weak legs, almost like I had forgotten how to walk…stumbling out of the alley, my chest heaving and I moaned as I struggled to breathe. As I made my way back to the tent, the only place I knew to go, I stared up at the bright moon, remembering a time I would smile as I contemplated the works of my Maker. But that night I felt nothing. Stumbling my way along the street back to the tent where it all started, I flung open the flap and gritted my teeth, glaring around in anger, anger at God, anger at my father for not protecting my mother… no… it was more than anger… it was blind rage."

This time, Alex clenched his fists and gritted his teeth as the memory of it all came flooding back. "I looked around the tent, through tear-stained eyes, my gaze running along the benches, still set up in their nice, little, neat rows. Taking the end of one in my hands, a scream escaped my mouth, as I flipped the large log end over end, the intense anger increasing my strength, as the log fell into the corner of the tent, nearly causing it to topple over. As tears blurred my vision, I made my way to the front of the makeshift church; the corner of the tent sagging as the fabric nearly brushed my head. I had foolishly believed in what my parents had talked about and lived, and believed it with my whole heart, all my mind… and now this is what it had cost me!"

Climbing the couple steps to the stage, I made my way to the front of the pulpit and gripped the wooden podium hard, my knuckles whitening as my fingers drove in the wood. Bowing my head with an attitude that was anything but reverent, my hair fell in front of my face in disarray, as spittle flew from my mouth. Reaching out toward a crucifix on the podium, I gripped it as tightly as I could in my fist, nearly crushing it as I cocked back my fist, sending the object flying toward the opening of the tent, like a softball, as it noisily clattered in the street. I fell to the ground in exhaustion, my hands balled into fists as pain screamed in my head. My mind struggled to remember things, to connect details, as if it was cloaked in a deep fog. It was almost as if I was being pulled by a current swimming through the rage that consumed me. My mind held onto the figure that I saw that night, running behind the thief. Samuel! I knew someone had to pay! My anger was seeking something to hold onto! I had no idea where the man who took the life of my mother had gone, but all I knew, at least, is where Samuel was. Before she was unfairly taken, I was a sincere, honest, but at times, impulsive, man. But, that night something in my life and in my heart snapped, just like that, and I never have been the same again...."

Chapter 11: Early morning, March 17, 1900

As he finished his story, he slowly turned to face Taylor, his dark eyes boring into her, as the two men on each side of her gripped her shoulders tighter, preventing her from escaping. "You see, my dear, my parents, both of them, died during that awful period… my mother, and then days later, I came home from playing with my friends in the street, to find my father slumped over the table, with empty bottles all around him, he had drank himself to death." His breathing slowed and he chose his next words very carefully, "My parents died then, but I also lost something else", as he walked slowly toward Taylor, a weak smile playing on his mouth, as he reached inside his coat pocket for something. "You see… I feel that, no wait, I don't feel anything anymore…. God did abandon me that day… now I know that everything my parents were saying during those meetings was nothing more than a crutch meant to make good people feel even better." With that, he withdrew the object in his pocket. A small, thin glass syringe, capped with a needle, was slowly revealed, causing Taylor to shudder, as a large hand closed over her mouth.

Alex walked slowly toward her, raising the syringe, and staring at it, a wicked smile coming across his lips. A clear liquid filled the syringe, as the man to her left, took her arm and held it down, against the arm of the chair. She violently pulled back, trying to wriggle free, but he held her arm in a vise-like grip. Alex very slowly walked toward her, his cane in one hand, the syringe in the other. "Do you know what this is, Taylor?" Taylor stayed as silent as the night outside the window. "Fine, I might as well let you know what will happen to you… First of all, I would like to say that your name… it has quite an interesting quality to it. In case you didn't know, it means just what it sounds like. A tailor is someone who fixes clothing, makes it fit. But you seem to be in too far now. I'm afraid you won't be able to fix this, you don't fit in here. And don't even think of trying anything, because you won't be getting out of here anytime soon either.

Now then…I just told you my life story, about the death of my parents…and how I lost something I can't get back… do you know what that is, that I'll never get back? Let me just say, first of all, your new husband is certainly quite the catch. I know his every move, what he does on weekends, the whole bit. I have been having my spies follow him for quite some time now. Rather an upstanding young man, I must say. There are two things I have noticed about him, though. Every Sunday, he attends services. Although sadly, it appears, this time, you'll have to miss that appointment", as he frowned mockingly.

"The other thing I've observed is that before every meal, and even before he goes to bed, he prays and reads his worn, leather, black Bible…how very noble". He said these last words slowly, he produced a worn, leather Bible from behind him, exactly like the one he had mentioned. "In other words, he has found hope, not the kind of hope that frail humans can offer, but the kind of hope my parents tried to give to others, the same kind of hope that eventually killed them. When they died, any hope I had inside of me, died with them. So…I have decided, after following your precious Samuel…", she cringed as this evil man uttered her husband's name, "… I have observed that he possesses in him, not just any hope, but a hope strong enough to change lives. What I neglected to tell you is that we both used to do that whole revival act together after all… we were close partners…" He dramatically paused for a short while, and then continued. "Oh, did I forget to mention that?" Alex cackled, as Taylor's eyes grew wide at this revelation.

Just then, the door to the apartment was thrown open as a thin young boy, not much older than twelve, stood breathing heavily. "Sir, I…I.., I did what y…you asked. But it, it w-wasn't e-enough. "What are you talking about?" asked Alex, rather irritated at this turn of events. "H…He is here…" Fear crept into Alex's voice as Taylor let out a shriek of joy, her eyes widening! "He's found me!! I told you. You will pay for this, you'll see!" Ignoring Taylor, Alex went over to the boy and motioned his accomplices over as well. In a low whisper, he ordered both of the men who had been holding Taylor down, "Ok, here's what I want you to do. Samuel's on his way. We need to delay him." Staring at the two men, he told them in a dark, menacing tone, "You go and take care of Samuel. Do what you have to, only leave him alive. Make sure he doesn't wake for a good while. I demand to know how he got here, and I want to know as soon as you find out."

Turning to the stockier of the two men, his eyes bore into the other man's intently. "As soon as he is conveniently delayed, I want you to take a pencil and some scrap paper, and write him a little message. Tell him how his precious Taylor won't be around to greet him. Make sure he doesn't know where this place is. Tell him that she died, rather, unfortunately. When he comes to, he'll see the note and he'll have to read it." Taylor struggled fiercely against her captors, "No! You can't do this! Please!" Alex walked over to her slowly, his footsteps echoing in the distance. Alex turned to face his friends, "I want to know how he got here, and I want to know now!"

In mid-stride, Alex was interrupted by the young boy. "Please sir, I think I know how he got here." "What is your name?" Alex ordered. "It's William, sir. I'm just a boy, turned ten just last week."

"Well then, speak up, boy!" screamed Alex.

"Yes sir", the boy stammered.

"I do remember a few months ago, a freighter came, docking into one of the nearby ports. I had come into town just about a half hour earlier. My family is poor, we don't have jobs, so I took to ridin' the rails, goin' from town to town, to see where I could get a job. Along the way, I couldn't find much, so I spent some times in those housing projects. Hoovervilles, I believe they were called. Anyways, I peered out the window of the train and stared at the freighter. This particular freighter seemed larger than any I had seen before. I picked up my bags and dashed to the front of the train. As the doors opened, I took the steps two at a time and sprinted across the platform. Bumping my way across the throngs of people, I flew over to the port, my eyes searching for the freighter I had seen. Soon, my eyes fell on it. I ran over as fast as my legs could carry me.

My heart thudding against my chest, I watched as the passengers filed down the walkway. I didn't have to wait long, though, only ten or so passengers could fit on the train, the boat was so small. After most of the passengers had departed, a young man with short blonde hair walked off the freighter, holding his bags. I looked up at him, knowing this must be Samuel. I asked him where he was going and what brought him here.

"One question at a time", he answered. "Will ya take my bags for me first? I'm tired"

Hesitantly I answered, "Sure". As we made our way to the nearest inn, I asked again, "So what you doing here, Samuel?"

I, uh, I... wait, how do ya know my name?"

"Never mind, it's not important", I answered.

Suspiciously, Samuel looked in my eyes and I cringed as he spoke again. "All right, I don't know who you are, but I just assumed you were a curious traveler, as I am. So since we're in the same predicament, I guess I gotta give you a chance. I live in Nebraska. It's a small town, but I enjoy it. I bought me a ticket to come across the ocean here and visit my cousin, haven't seen her since I was a kid."

"What's her name?" the young boy asked.

"Her name is Meghan, got a sister named Ashley too. They're twins, real tough to tell em apart." He laughed. "Hope I know which one is which", he grinned. "I'm sure you'll do fine", the youngster assured him. In a more serious tone, Samuel added, "I was told my wife had a sister out here as well. Being overseas, news doesn't travel too fast so I'm afraid she hasn't heard the unfortunate news yet. My wife is apparently very ill. I just got a telegram the other day. I wanna do nothing more than go back home, and be by her side, but there's no freighters going back that way for a while. It's gonna be rough to tell her. I never was good at breaking terrible news, but it's gotta be done, I'm afraid. She just got married too."

"What's your wife's sister's name?' the boy asked.

"Not sure, but I believe it's Jaylee", replied Samuel. The youth wasn't sure whether to believe Samuel's story or not, but since he didn't have anything else to go on, he didn't have a choice. The young boy said to Alex quickly, "It was nice meeting you. I got somewhere I gotta go right now. Wait here, I'll return soon."

"Uh, ok. Guess I can wait for a bit." Samuel said.

The youngster made his way back to where Alex and the other men were. Panting for breath, he leaned his hands on his knees, stammering, "He's claimed to visiting his cousin. His wife also had a sister he was gonna go and visit as well. Guess his wife has fallen ill. He needs to go back home and be with her, but no freighters going back that way for a while. His story seems to check out. Don't have any reason not to believe him." He held his hand out to Alex, "Do I get paid now?"

"Paid?" Alex laughed. "No, you don't. I need you to go back to the freight yard," he ordered the young boy.

"Why?' he asked.

I have information that he goes there every evening. The waves are relaxing for him, he sits on one of the barges and reads that Bible of his. He finds some sort of odd comfort in it. You'll find him there. If you can meet him sooner, that would be even better, though" Pointing to another of the stocky men in his group, he lowered his voice, "Go with him. He's gonna need help. Don't take anything, remember, do what you have to, I just need him alive." The man nodded and ran after the boy. The boy called back, "I was walking with him to get something for dinner. Can we do that first?"

"Ok, fine", Alex said, exasperated. "But I think I know where he has in mind. It's the best place in town. We'll be waiting. We've gotta catch him before he goes to meet his sister. If he does go and meet her, we'll lose him for sure then." Alex and the other men smiled wickedly.

The young boy made his way back to Samuel, soon finding him in a crowded part of town. "Glad to see you are back", Samuel told his new friend. Holding out a Bible, he offered it to the boy. "No thanks", the boy said.

"Suit yourself", Samuel shrugged his shoulders. "Every night I go to the docks and sit facing the shore. I read this Bible, watching the waves roll in. You should try it sometime. It is quite relaxing. Gives me plenty of chances to think about things, life and stuff."

"I know you do", William muttered under his breath.

"What was that?", Samuel asked curiously. William shrugged his shoulders, "Oh nothing, he said" In response, Samuel remained silent.

Walking past the shipyard, they saw the apartments in the distance. Samuel's eyes widened as he turned excitedly to his new friend. "Let's go to those apartments! But first, I'm starving, and there's supposed to be a fantastic restaurant around there somewhere. Not sure where it is, but we're bound to find it if we just keep looking. It's still early, we got plenty of time." The young boy outwardly groaned, mumbling his disapproval as they walked closer to the apartments. Turning his head downward, he smiled wickedly as they walked closer to the apartments, his hands fumbling in his pockets.

Samuel ran closer to the apartment buildings when his ears picked up a very faint, high, terrified voice! Just then, a gust of wind blew through, muffling the voice. 'It sounds like the wind, but...', his thought trailed off as the aroma of delicious food traveled over him. As he ran closer to the smell of food drifting through the city, he crossed a dark alley. At the same instant, a fist caught him unaware, directly across his cheek,, sending him sprawling to the alley! Two figures got their hands under his shoulders and put a handkerchief drenched in chloroform over his face, dragging him into the darkness. "That should do it", whispered the muscular man to the young boy. Pulling a letter from his pocket, he dropped it, sending it fluttering down to the alley. He picked up the letter and patted the man's breast pocket, putting it inside. "This should explain everything", he whispered.

    Hours later, Samuel whimpered in pain, as he struggled to move, finally managing to stretch his arm out slightly. Brilliant colors danced around his vision and he turned face down to empty his stomach. As his fingers began wrapping around a piece of paper, he heard faint squeaking noises in the distance! He struggled to open his eyes, but they had swollen shut. He wasn't sure how long he'd been out. Reaching down he patted his breast pocket and felt something inside. The telltale crumple of paper! Must be a note of some sort! Blindly, he pulled it out and tried to open his eyes just enough to read, but it was no use. He tried to search his memory for any clues to what had happened to him. The last thing he remembered was walking with a young boy to grab something to eat. He passed an alley, and that was all he remembered…no, he did remember one final thing. It was on the very edges of his memory. As he remembered walking, he had heard a scream! It was very faint, and the wind had nearly drowned it out! Samuel struggled to stay awake as he tried to put the pieces of the puzzle together, but soon he surrendered as his head flopped back in a puddle of water, the note clutched tightly in his hand, his only lifeline to the world outside.

    Taylor began carefully sorting through the

confusion. "So, you knew Samuel was coming, and you had him followed", Taylor screamed at Alex, as the young boy finished his story. "Then, you figured out his habits and used them against him! He was making his way to the restaurant, totally innocent, and you just beat him up! And then wrote a letter, telling him that I had died? He will be heartbroken, knowing he couldn't be at my side! You are a very cruel, bitter man! God will punish you!"

"You don't seem to understand yet, my dear. I have lived in the shadow of your husband for far too long! It's time that I have my day in the sun! And whatever I must do to make that happen, I will! When I lost my parents, my view of everything good and perfect, my view of God Himself, became muddled and murky. There is no hope in this world unless it's what we make of it! That's what has become clear to me! And while your precious Samuel has, or had, his life divinely laid out for him, I had it all ripped away from me! Don't you understand, I needed to be important! I needed to feel loved again! But now any feelings of belonging and purpose I would have had are completely gone!

"Belonging, purpose, love and acceptance... in a word, hope. That was what was meant for me, but it was stolen that night, so long ago, so I suppose I shall have to steal someone else's, so to speak...After observing you two, so young and in love, the world by the tail...I have come to the conclusion that the emotion of love is the strongest reason for hope. When you love someone, you would cross the highest mountain, brave the strongest storm, to be with them, would you not?" Taylor shivered as she finally understood what was happening.

"Now, finally onto the business of what is in this vial. Have you ever heard of tuberculosis? Surely you must... I suppose you may have, or even know friends who have been infected with it…Oh, it is a dreaded disease… as of now, there's no cure for it. I don't suppose there will ever be a cure. So here's what's going to happen to you next… I have a vial of the disease in this syringe, and I am going to inject all of it into your arm in a matter of minutes. Don't you worry though, you won't feel a thing, because I will give you something to put you to sleep first.… my trusted, yet misguided accomplice here.…", he pointed his cane at the young man who first was with him in the room, "as I have warned you already, has already broken the heartbreaking news to your precious husband, that you had an rather unfortunate brush with the disease and died quickly, but peacefully, unlike most of the poor victims. He's out like a light now, but don't worry, he'll be up soon, and when he does, I've left a letter with him, explaining everything." Taylor looked at him in disgust, seething with anger.

Oh, and I am glad you didn't waste your breath on trying to convince him not to. I have already informed him that if he wasn't willing to obey my orders, things would definitely end… rather badly for him. You see, he loves his dear profession, entirely too much I should think, and anyway, I am sure he couldn't survive the consequences of his disobedience, should he go against my orders. But that's not for you to worry about… And please don't try to escape, I would hate to make things worse and go after you. Now, let's go over this once more, shall we? I'm going to try to put this in words you'll understand, he said, holding up a book of fairy tales. Taylor recoiled in horror as she recognized the book given to her by her mother!

"This," he said, grandly motioning around the small,

modest room, "is my apartment". In one corner, a small desk stood, beside it, a soft bed. Nothing else could be found, besides those. "But I'd like you to think of it as a tower. It's two stories, sort of like a tower. Now then, you are to play the part of the princess locked in the tower. And I am the evil villain who has captured the princess, and now she aches for her dashing prince to come in and save the day, as he no doubt will try to do. How romantic! You may even say that I am a dragon. I do indeed have the heart of one. Everyone knows a dragon's most vulnerable point is his heart.

"You need a change of heart, is what you need!" Taylor interrupted. "No, I don't think that's what the problem is. I'm just protecting what is mine! Power, greed and desire! Every dragon needs a treasure to protect. The only problem that you face though is your dear prince won't be saving you this time. Not only that, but he will lose the two things he has fought so hard to keep, and I daresay he would die for; his hope and his precious maiden. He doesn't have to die though; all you have to do is tell him to call off the silly, useless search for his friend. If you fail to do that, it appears you will die in his place after all, sort of a sacrifice. And I... well; I will finally have my vengeance...." Taylor spoke what she was afraid could possibly be her final words on this earth, in as defiant a manner as she could manage, despite her growing fear, "You'll never win!! Samuel will find me again... you don't know him as well as I do, you have no idea...He will cross the ends of the earth to see me again..."

"Silence!!" Alex bellowed angrily, as the thump of his cane echoed loudly through the darkness of the room. His voice softened as he spoke to her a second time, "I have only one more thing to say to you, before we both have to leave, in different ways, of course. These fairy tales I've spoken of, my parents used to read them to me, as well, just different versions. Before the Brothers Grimm, who were the ones responsible for writing them and telling them, before they wrote the more popular versions, there existed... darker... versions. None of those had the 'happily ever afters', that we are all so used to. I won't burden you with those details, though. Considering the mess you find yourself in, surely they would make your skin crawl. My parents told me those versions to make life realistic, make me more of a man! It's not all hope and love and faith. There's real evil, real darkness. But then, I suppose life isn't full of happy endings, now is it? Your precious husband, as I have already said, has the power to ignite hope in people. I've seen it in his eyes...and as we both know, every hero needs his dragon, every savior must carry their cross...after all, evil cannot thrive without good, nor can good exist without evil", his voice faded off, as at the same time, the man holding her arm plunged the liquid deep in her veins. Her vision swam and she became groggy as her body grew limp, her tongue swelling as she was unable to get out another word. Trying to gather her thoughts enough for one final scream, her thoughts were too jumbled to know what to do.

After pulling the needle slowly from her arm, he capped the syringe. Taylor slumped roughly to the floor, her hair neatly arrayed around her head like the halo of angel; her still form appearing as if in a deep sleep. Alex then roughly took his accomplice by the arm, returning the syringe safely to his pocket. He spoke a final time, staring intently at her figure on the floor once more, feigning sadness, dabbing his eyes with a handkerchief, to complete his act. "I am so very sorry, I had such high hopes for you… but don't worry, no one will never know what happened here", as the two men walked toward the door, the cane eerily echoing on the wooden floor. Alex carefully twisted the glass doorknob and looking back once again, smiling as they disappeared without a trace, into the warm, muggy night. Taylor lay helplessly on the cold, wooden floor, her chest slowly rising and falling with each breath she took.

    After what seemed like forever, Taylor blinked her eyes through a thick haze, craning her neck just enough to get a look at her surroundings. A wooden desk lay in the far right corner of the room. A small cot lay just in front of that. She was lying on a wooden floor, in a room which she judged to be roughly twelve feet long by thirty six feet in length. She struggled to prop herself on her elbow, but lost her balance as her weak arm gave out under her. Before her head dropped to the floor, she barely noticed a small, commonplace door with peeling white paint. The knob showed signs of rust and wear as well. She struggled to breathe, the warm air making her draw in large gasps, as she looked up to the frame of the windows, noticing they were peeling as well. A cool draft of air hit her, as she realized that, in his rush, Samuel had neglected to close the windows, allowing her access to vital air and possibly saving her life in the process. Fighting through the confusion sweeping through her, she struggled to crawl over to the far wall, and once she had made her way over slowly, placed her hands on a metal pipe, struggling to pull herself up, in an attempt to attract attention. She managed to get her unsteady feet under her briefly, just long enough to summon a hidden reserve of strength, as every muscle in her body screamed for relief. She banged three times roughly on the window, hoping anyone would hear her. As she banged the third time, her legs buckled underneath her and she slid to the floor, too weak to move. Her body was drenched in sweat; her hair plastered to her face. Outside the building, people slept in the nearby apartments, homeless children running along the streets, trying to ignore the heat; completely ignorant of the awful events of this night.

Except for one small boy named William. This young, nine year old child was walking along through an alley beside the place where Taylor lay, when he heard three loud knocks against a window, a muffled scream, and then silence. Startled, he dropped the coins he had been carrying for his father. He had been standing in the food line for them, as they were poor and needed bread. He backpedaled in the direction he had come, fighting against the tide of people coming the other way. He ran as fast as his legs could carry him, nearly knocking a policeman off his feet. As they practically crashed into each other, William pulled to a stop and looked up into the face of the man. Struggling for breath, he explained, "Please sir... I... heard... a woman... I think... rapping against the window... She's.... in trouble... needs help...".

He put his hand against his knees, pointing up to the second floor of the building. The policeman, a kind blonde haired man named Donald, followed his gaze, opening his mouth, as he faintly saw a tightly closed fist rap once more against the window, as if in slow motion, then watched as her figure fell, fading from sight. The policeman blew on his whistle and threw it down in disgust when he realized the rest of his men were across town, probably having breakfast or some such thing. It had seemed like a quiet morning a minute ago, so he decided to give them some time off. He really wished now that he hadn't done that. "You done good here, William. I reckon there's a reward in it for you."

"Thank you sir, but I ain't interested in no reward. I only done it cause I seen she needed help and I knew that I couldn't just stand by and watch." William bravely said, though his voice shook slightly. The policeman handed William a few coins for his trouble anyway, and they ran to the apartment building. "This was a good thing you've done here. But see, I've told my men that they could have time off today. Figured it would be a slow day, and nothing would happen. But now that I'm here without any help, and we got someone in need of our assistance, I'm gonna appoint you my deputy for the day. Think you can handle that, William? Just do as I say and we'll catch the person who did this." William nodded nervously, "Yes sir." Donald responded, "That's a good boy. Now just do what I tell ya to, and you'll do fine." William's palms were caked with sweat as he and the policeman made their way up to the door of the building. The policeman turned the knob roughly in his hands, wiping away sweat, and pulled with all his might, but it wouldn't budge. Finally he stood back and kicked the door roughly. The aged door gave way as wood splintered. With a few more well placed kicks, the policeman ran in as the door fell to the ground with a mighty crash! There, in the corner of the room, a figure lay huddled and helpless on the floor, her knees up to her chest and her arms around her tight. He knelt down and put his arms under her shoulders, dragging her away from the wall, as her head lolled to one side. He craned his head down to put his ear to her lips, she was just barely breathing, but alive, thank the Lord!

Just then, William and the policeman heard loud footsteps, followed by the cocking action of a rifle! Donald grabbed the boy's arm roughly, "Quick, there's a blanket in the corner! Hide there, and don't you move!" William ran over to the corner as the policeman held his breath. Staying as quiet as he could, he heard the footsteps gradually get closer. He really wished now that he had brought more than just his club to defend himself with! He looked out of the corner of his eye to see the blanket, laying on the floor, William underneath it, breathing very slow and evenly. The doorknob turning slowly, Donald thought quickly and at the last instant, ran to the other side of the room, pulling the window shut! The rush of air was the only thing that had saved Taylor, maybe shutting the window could work to his advantage! It was a very warm morning, one that made him want to strip to his undershirt. But, if they did succeed in this, he needed his clothes and his badge.

The door creaked open slowly and the barrel of a shotgun slowly revealed itself! Alex stepped into the apartment and wrapped his hands tighter around the stock. Donald hid behind the door, as it opened, and took a deep breath as he slowly walked forward, the boards creaking under his feet! Bringing his arm back, he swung his club with all his might, straight at Alex's neck! The blow would have been enough to finish him off, had he not turned at the last instant.

The blow struck him full in the cheek, the force of the impact swinging the gun toward the direction of the huddled figure in the blanket, causing his gun to go off! Donald jumped aside as the impact caught him in the hip, sending him crumpling to the ground! At the same instant the bullet its target, William threw off his cover and ran headlong into Alex. As William bravely rushed into Alex, he threw his fists, blows landing wherever he could get to. Donald briefly smiled, admiring the boy's courage.

Donald placed his hands on the floor, trying to bring himself to his feet, but it was no use! Donald realized in horror that something was terribly wrong! Screaming in agony, he tried again to push himself up off the floor, grunting with the effort. His legs fell limp and useless behind him, the muscled in his arms straining as he tried in vain to scoot toward the door. He screamed for William through his tears, but his new friend was too full of rage at the moment to do anything. The last thought Donald remembered having was when his wife and kids helped him to celebrate his birthday last year. Even though he knew that they loved him dearly, he had no idea what they would think of him now. He didn't want them or anyone to see him like this! After grabbing onto the bottom of the windowsill, he screamed with effort, attempting to bring himself up one final time, hoping against hope that this was all a bad dream. As his eyes swam with color, his head finally slumped to the floor and he blacked out, amid the shouts of Alex and William.

A short time later, he wasn't aware of just how long, he awoke. Out of the corner of his eye, still against the ground, he saw Alex on all fours, struggling for breath. "Get off of me!", he managed to mutter as William clung to him desperately, his fists pummeling Alex's body and William screaming for all he was worth, the sweat poured off them both. Alex finally managed to grab William by the shoulders and push him away, causing him to stumble and hit the floor. Staggering toward the desk, he placed both his hands down on it and drew in thick gulps of air. This was his chance to finally do something! Seeing his partner lying helpless on the floor, William summoned up reserves of strength he didn't even know he had, wrapping a hand around Alex's midsection and slapped the cuffs around one wrist before Alex had a chance to react! Before he could take his other arm from the desk, William pulled Alex's arm back roughly, nearly tearing it from the socket. He quickly cuffed Alex's hands together and shoved him roughly through the open door. Donald craned his neck and smiled weakly, impressed by this young boy's display of bravery and hidden strength. 'His parents must be so proud of him', thought Donald.

As sweat poured off both their faces, a man came jogging up to them, carrying a police whistle, wearing an official uniform. "Came runnin' fast as I could!" William looked at him impatiently, trying to act brave, "Yeah, uh, thanks. We're done here, though." The man's eyes widened as he looked over to his injured captain, his eyes softening. "I'm sorry, boss...I wasn't here..." Donald looked at him, as William shoved Alex roughly toward him. "Just get him booked, and read him his rights." he breathed heavily, his voice showing no emotion. Donald said, with disappointment in his voice, his hair matted to his forehead, exhausted from trying to stand. "Listen, I don't know... where the rest of the force is. I gave them... a day off and I shouldn't have...had I known that something... like this... would happen. I just need someone to book the prisoner. Can you do that for me? I never meant for you to see me like this. Now, please leave. Don't you worry, now. I'll be fine here. Someone will hear us. Just get outta here!." With sadness in his eyes, his friend turned and walked off, pushing Alex roughly ahead of him.

As his buddy left him alone, he turned toward Taylor,

looking at her, eyes full of compassion, "We're both hurt, but I can't be fussin' about myself right now. I reckon I'll have plenty of time for that from now on. Right now, I gotta make sure you're gonna be alright. Help is comin' soon, I won't leave you till they come! We found the person that did this to you, and he's going away a long time, I promise you." He knelt down and pulled her over to the door, and using his free hand, reached up to pound roughly on the door, using his whistle to summon for more help. Yelling until his voice was hoarse, he leaned down to whisper once more in her ear, "Hang on there, help is on the way! I'm not leavin' you, you have my word!"

Chapter 12: May 3, 1930

Approximately a mile and a half in each direction from where Yo-Yo was fighting off the grasshoppers, an old worn farmhouse settled in the middle of an intersection of dusty trails. A wooden fence served as a boundary for the property, as well as giving a home to the dozen or so chickens, mice, and a goat or two. In the far left corner of the property, a lone, rusty windmill sat completely still, a sure sign that the destruction of the environment had not yet come this far.

This farmhouse looked like every other farmhouse around these parts, except for one important difference. Where the animals were usually crying for food or bleating for no apparent reason, all the animals on this farm were completely quiet. No chickens pecked the ground, no goats bleated for food, not even the sound of a mouse scurrying could be heard. A sense of fear and dread covered the entire area, even though, at this moment, the sun was still shining, giving the occupants inside a false sense of hope and security.

Two people, an older man and a woman, with about fifteen years or so separating them, sat quietly at the kitchen table. Both had their hands folded before them, though not in prayer. As they both stared down at the table for the longest time, the older woman, Taylor, was the first to speak. "I...I still don't understand... You lied to him!" The man responded in a kind, but stern voice. "No.... remember, I told him what he needed to hear, considering the circumstances! I told you this was coming!" he exclaimed as he stood up quickly, the chair falling to the ground. The man continued on, "Now, let's think about this, surely we can come to a reasonable solution. After all, I know I threatened you with that awful disease all those years ago, but, unless I am mistaken, you're still here, are you not?"

Taylor spoke up quickly as her words cut like a knife through the humid air, "A reasonable solution, there is nothing reasonable about what you did! What you did to me, to my poor husband, and most of all, to his poor horse, the only thing he owned, who loved him unconditionally, and who's now out there all alone, who knows where, and you are to blame!"

The man, who was named Alex, the very same man who stole Yo-Yo away all those months ago, and threatened Taylor long ago, raised his hands in protest. He reached in his pocket, pulling out a couple of bills.

Taylor yelled, "Stop, just, please stop! You think money is an answer for everything! But I don't need your money…! You tried to pay me off for keeping quiet about Yo-Yo! And I didn't say a word, but I was at the farm the day Samuel's only friend was taken. I had just got home from meeting an old friend in the nearest town, and I heard you two talking. I ran into the house to stay hidden, noticing a scrap of paper with a note on it. It read 'Don't say a word about what you hear', and beside it were a couple bills, enough to keep me going for a short while. As I strained my ears to hear, I listened as I heard his poor horses' name come up. Samuel started crying and pleading with you! I knew then that things were going to end badly. I tried to listen but I couldn't hear much. The next thing I knew, a door slammed and the truck drove away! I peered out from the corner of the house and will never forget what I saw next! My poor husband was kneeling in the dirt and crying loudly. I heard the helpless neighs of Yo-Yo in the distance, and I wanted so bad to rush over to Samuel! But he already thought I was dead! I knew he wouldn't survive the shock of his only friend being taken away, then immediately seeing his wife he thought was dead. So against my better judgment, I took your money, and left, vowing to return to him again. Don't you see, nothing can change what you've done…"

Alex slowly put the money back in his pocket, and placing his hands on the table, took a slow, deep breath. "Trust me, this was the only way. I told you I needed to have my vengeance, and believe me, his poor horse wasn't in the agreement, but it had to be done. But now that it is, we can start completely over, move you to a place far from here and who knows, maybe you will see your family again.

In the meantime, a buggy is leaving for Chicago early in the morning. I suggest you take the money I gave you, pack up your things and get on it.. Once you get there, I gave a lifelong friend of mine fair warning you were coming. She can let you use the top floor of her apartment; it is very nicely furnished, everything you need is there. Our country is going downhill, Taylor, along with the economy, we need to start over. What happened in the past, I realize my mistakes cost me more than I know, what has happened to everyone else, the crash, the storms, and everything… has caused me to think about things…"

"Please ," Taylor cried, her face buried in her hands, her gray hair, once a brilliant blonde, falling from the bun in her hair. Her voice shook as she spoke… "What you said just now, about leaving and starting over…I will admit that times haven't been the best lately, and I do want things to get better, but running away from all this," her hands spread out to encompass the land around them, "is not the answer. Don't try to apologize. It's too late for that. And you know what the worst thing is? The very worst thing is," her fist shook as she pointed a finger in his face, "was telling my poor husband I had died! Do you know what that did to him, to us? I couldn't even be there that horrible day! His heart must have been breaking a million times over, and I was nowhere around to comfort him! I knew then that I wasn't in any danger of dying, and I wanted nothing more than to contact him, but in my foolishness and greed I took your dirty money as payment for staying quiet, you made me think I had no choice, but now I wish I never had! Nothing is more important to me than my family, and I promise you, I will see them again, in this life or the next…"

"I admire your courage", said Alex quietly. "But you have to understand as well, we are living in times where a man has to pull himself up by his own bootstraps. We here have been spared from everything this far, but who knows how much longer we have? I suggest you get on the first buggy to come through in the morning, move to Chicago, take all your things, and start anew. That way, if you do see your family again, and you must believe me, I sincerely hope you do, you will have a new home and new surroundings in which to raise them. They deserve better than what they have now, do they not?" Taylor's voice was soft as she spoke, "Yes, they do, and maybe there is some truth to what you are saying, but I still can't trust you.….I won't…"

The next day was very bleak and dark as Taylor prepared for the trip to the big city. She angrily snatched her clothes from the closet and began putting them inside a thick suitcase. Staring out at the cloudless day, she began thinking about her conversation with Alex last night, as well as that dark day, many lifetimes ago, it now seemed. Some people have no heart! He was going to pay for what he did! In that moment, when revenge seemed the best and only option, she remembered something her mother had told her long ago. When you take revenge on someone, you had better be ready to dig two graves, one for the other person and another for yourself. That made perfect sense, actually. Her next thought then was that the best revenge she could take was to show Alex that she could survive, no matter what happened to her.

A daring plan came to her mind next, one that not even Alex could ruin. But she knew she couldn't do it on her own. She would need some unique help. Fortunately, her mother long ago, when she was just a little girl, took her to church and the preacher constantly gave sermons of how the Lord is in control of all things and how, when wicked men do evil things, that revenge belongs to the Lord and not to men. As she finished packing and pulled the zipper tight around the suitcase, the last thing she remembered was a young man telling her once that people these days had to pull themselves up by their own bootstraps, just like Alex had told her.

Little did they know that the One she took orders from had feet that were stronger, whose sandals had once walked upon this earth, and who ached for mankind to depend on Him, so he could display his love to them and form a relationship with His creation. He knew pain, loneliness, abandonment and treachery, just as she did. Her plan at that moment was set. She would willingly move to Chicago, live in the apartment for a while and become an important member of society, maybe work at a newspaper office. After she answered an ad for a good job, she would work there for a while, as long as she needed to, and then she would go looking for her family, and once she found them, they would move far away. She could only hope and pray that, God willing, they were both alright.

Miles away, as Yo-Yo sat in the wagon, cringing from what he had just seen, but strangely calmed by the effect of the man's words, he lay there thinking in silence, the swarm of grasshoppers having no effect on him as the men yanked open the crate and unscrewed the bottles of what he found out later was banana oil, by the color of it and what the men said about it. They began slowly pouring it around the perimeter of the wagon. Little did anyone know at that time, that the events of the past hour, both here and miles away in the old farmhouse, would change Yo-Yo's fate forever.

Chapter 13: May 5, 1930

One day, both Samuel and Nathaniel made their way over to the same canyon where they had rescued the calf. Harnessing their horses to a couple of sturdy trees, they made their way frantically on foot to the edge of the ravine. As they ran along the outer edge, their eyes downcast, Nathaniel said with fear in his voice, "It must be here! It has to be! My ring, it fell off somewhere here, during the rescue, we've gotta find it! It's all I have to remember my wife by!" "How did it happen?" Samuel asked gently. "I don't know! I guess it must have fallen outta my pocket during the storm, looking for my calf! When my wife passed away, I didn't care to wear it no more, filled with grief as I was, so I put it away in my shirt pocket. I didn't have the heart to put it away fer good, I still needed to have it close. Anyways, I got arthritis real awful; my joints are all swollen, so I had to stick it in my shirt pocket, couldn't wear it again even if I wanted to… Oh, we just gotta find it!" Samuel laid a hand on his friend's bony shoulder, "It's ok, I understand, and we'll find it! I know all too well what you are going through!" Samuel turned to the right, the large, loose rocks tumbling down, as the landscape sloped down, into a lazy, meandering river. Suddenly, and without any warning, another intense dust storm kicked up out of nowhere! Running around in a panic as the dust pelted their faces, they were forced to their knees as the wind pushed them off balance. Luckily, they were still able to see a short distance. Then, just as suddenly as it had begun, the storm lessened.

As the intense storm died down, Samuel and Nathaniel

stared off into the distance, as a thick cloud of insects swarmed across them. In a short time, everything was covered, as thousands of grasshoppers, some larger than others, clung to everything, the rocks, the horses, and even Samuel and Nathaniel themselves were covered with so many of the bugs; it was extremely difficult to see. Samuel let out a yelp as a dozen bugs jumped on his skin, causing him to drop the tin can. His muscles straining, he held on tightly to the rope, as a few of the insects veered off from the rest of the swarm and completely enveloped the rope. Their segmented bodies totally covering it, Nathaniel had no choice but to use his hand to shoo away some of the unwanted invaders. "We gotta get outta here now!" Nathaniel shouted down to Samuel, above the racket. As Samuel gazed nervously up the sheer wall of the cliff, he knew that he had to get up there himself or neither of them would make it out at all.

With the rope still lying on the ground, with enough length to wrap it firmly around his waist, he picked it up quickly, throwing the rope above his head as he slammed it on the ground to get rid of some of the insects, watching some of them scatter. Staring up, Samuel gave the rope a quick tug, knowing that Nathaniel had secured it already. Even though they were getting up in years, both men were still strong and had life left in them yet. Closing his eyes and praying softly, Samuel reached above his head, finding a handhold to grab. As he grunted with exertion, he raised his free hand and unconsciously swiped his hand around him. A puzzled look came over his face as he realized suddenly there was nothing to swipe away! As his feet found another hold, he looked briefly behind him to see the massive swarm still in the canyon, very aggressive, but where he was, and a couple feet all around him, was nothing but air. Something, or someone, had caused the insects to stay away from him long enough for him to get up the cliff face! Samuel quickly made his way further up the side of the rock; unsure of how much longer his luck would last, knowing that his good fortune, at least for the moment, was due to much more than just luck.

Halfway up the cliff, Samuel could hear Nathaniel screaming, as he tried to get the insects away. Samuel sighed, as he knew he had to get up to his friend quickly. Grunting loudly, he made his way the last few feet up to his friend. Reaching above him, every muscle protesting, he pushed his way over the cliff onto the ground. Allowing himself only a couple minutes' rest, he stood up slowly, his hands reaching into his pockets for anything he could find that might help them. His hands closing around a small bottle, he smiled wide to himself. Fishing in his other pocket, he wrapped his bony fingers around a slim, but large cloth bag. Untying the drawstring from the bag, he struggled to draw a breath. As he pulled open the bag quickly, he looked inside as relief flooded his face.

Inside the bag were hundreds of tiny pellets of grain. Pulling out three of the bottles with his left hand, he set them upon the rocks, covering them with a handkerchief so they would be safe from the grasshoppers. Reaching out to grab the tin can, he started to pour the contents of the bottles inside the tin can, when he suddenly stopped. He remembered he had punched an opening in the bottom of the can, in order to run a string through and serve as a makeshift walkie talkie. But he groaned in frustration as he realized that the howling wind wouldn't allow him to talk clear, rendering that plan useless. Tearing a corner from his shirt, he wadded the cloth up and stuffed it into the hole tight, so none of the contents would run out. Satisfied that the opening was securely plugged; he began to unscrew the caps from the bottles, one by one, pouring them into the can until the liquid came about half an inch from the top.

After the liquid was completely emptied into the can, he took the small bottles and stuffed them into his coat pocket, because nothing was to be wasted. Finding the sack of grain pellets in his other pocket; he untied the drawstring and opened the sack, careful not to lose any of the pellets. Quickly moving the sack over above the tin can, he carefully emptied the pellets into the liquid. A man that he had met, long ago, had taught him this trick. The liquid he had stored up in the glass bottles was banana oil, a man-made liquid, with the unmistakable scent of bananas, but that was their only similarity to the fruit.

Samuel was glad he had these bottles with him, because aside from being a farmer, which was in itself a full-time job, he, along with all these other men, also made soaps and sold them to their neighbors, a task for which the banana oil was very necessary. He had been doing that for only a few months, but he knew just enough to get by. It never did pay much at all, in fact, nowadays, it didn't pay anything.

Pulling a small branch from a nearby tree, he stirred the contents of the bag carefully, not spilling a drop. As soon as the mixture was completely mixed, he closed the bag and stepped back a few steps. Dumping the mixture on the rocks, he scattered it from one end of the ledge to the other, forming a dividing line between them and the insects. All they could do now was wait and hope this would work. As the relentless grasshoppers crawled up the face of the cliff in massive swarms, their bodies crawling over one another to get the men, they slowly moved closer to the banana oil.

As their bodies reached the sticky concoction, they slowed their march, and suddenly stopped. A slow smile spread over Samuel and Nathaniel's faces as they realized it had worked! The banana oil acted as poison for the insects, just long enough so they could mount their horses and get away. They quickly got on their horses and were just about to snap the reins, when Nathaniel noticed a shiny object glinting sharply off the sunlight, as it lay firmly between two small circular shaped rocks. Nathaniel flew off his horse and ran over to the ring, picked it up and let out a whoop of joy, as a big smile covered his face. Placing it securely on his finger, he got back on the horse and they both continued their escape, spurring the horses on as fast as they could, not caring where they went.

As the horses flew past the dense brush, out of the canyon, the landscape changed slowly back to farmland as the rocky spires gave way to gentle sloping hills, which soon gave way to barren fields once again. Samuel looked over his shoulder as he noticed Nathaniel struggling to keep up with him, the insects threatening to overtake him as he struggled to swat them away with his free hand. Samuel looked at the sky as thick swarms followed closely behind, "Hang on! We're almost there! I see a farmhouse just up ahead, we'll find shelter there!"

As the farmhouse came within sight, they pulled back sharply on the horses' reins and, nearly jumping from their mounts; practically fell over each other, as they swung the door open. As they flew into the house, they looked around to see an old man and woman standing at opposite sides of the room, hands folded against their chests. Pleading with the woman, he said, "You need to close your windows and plug up any sort of opening in this house. Use rags or anything you have with you! I don't have time to explain, just do it NOW!"

As Taylor and Alex ran around the house closing the windows violently, and tearing off rags to plug up any holes, she turned briefly to stare at the man in front of her, older but still just as handsome, she noticed, as a flash of recognition crossed her face. She froze where she stood as she left Alex to finish fortifying the homestead. The dishtowel she was carrying nearly dropped to the floor as her other hand flew to her mouth in disbelief.

In a soft whisper, she murmured, "I.... I can't believe....How is it possible?"

"Ma'am, are you all right?" Samuel asked slowly, his eyes locked on hers, unable to tear his gaze away. His lip trembled, sensing something strangely familiar about her face, though it was changed by time and circumstances. After a few minutes of silence, his eyes too, widened, as tears streamed down his cheeks. He walked slowly toward her, his vision blurry. "But…....how can you… be here? I thought….you were dead? The note... "

Samuel walked slowly up to this beautiful woman, placing his shaking hands on her warm cheeks. Her heart melted as he leaned forward and pulled her close to him, in a loving, protective embrace. He carefully placed a soft, gentle kiss on her warm lips, stroking her cheek softly. His hands were still shaking as he pulled his face away gently; gazing into her soft, gentle eyes. "Remember as children we used to love the fairy tales our parents would read us?" Smiling wide enough that he was sure his face would crack in two, he leaned to her again, and whispered, "Your prince has come, my dear, and I won't ever leave you again." Pulling away, Taylor fished in her pockets for something. Samuel stared at her curiously, as she pulled a ring from her pocket. Samuel's eyes widened in shock, "Where... how... did you... find it?"

Taylor's next words were slow and gentle, "I saw you the day your precious horse was taken. I know what it did to you, how it hurt you and left you lost and desperate. You looked so broken, so hopeless. I wasn't about to let you go. I figured your next move would be to try and win another one, seeing as how you still had crops and all. I came right before you, the day you noticed that flayer about the poker game. I knew what you were gonna do, you always were the impulsive one." Samuel blushed to hear her say that. "So I went over to the saloon, and asked the sheriff for a room. Taylor shuddered as she remembered his response, "H..he told me, 'Sure, for a pretty young thing like you..'" "That made me nearly sick, it did!

"I paid for a room, but I traded some of my belongings for a rifle, just in case. I stayed up there till the day of the tournament came. When it started, I sat down on a stool and just talked with some ladies workin; there, but you have to know that all the while my heart was achin' for you. I looked over and seen you and it took all I had to keep the tears from comin'. As the game kept on, I known the sheriff was a cheat and a liar.

"I seen him switch hands with you and his other men. Then I saw him up the stakes. What a nasty move that was, knowing you had to bet the only thing you had left! When I seen you pull out the wedding ring, that sent me over the edge! I ran to the bathroom and just knelt down and cried! I knew it wasn't your fault!

John made you do it! Don't blame yourself! He's an evil man. Well, I hid till the game was over and you had left, so had most of the patrons. John left to flirt with one of the ladies and left the ring on the table! Well, fortunately no one seen me, them being drunk and all, so I snatched it up and I ran outta there as if the devil himself were after me!

I got on a horse that was tied up, and I ran it as far as I could. I made quite the commotion, but the Lord Himself coulda come down then and they wouldn't have known. I knew you were still heartbroken about Yo-Yo, so I couldn't risk the surprise of you seeing me yet! I had to wait for what I thought would be the right time! And then, Alex..." she shuddered at his name. He...he kidnapped me; he had me held for what seemed a long time. I started to believe that I'd never escape, oh, it was so very awful! I wanted to find you, but he told me never to escape. I was so afraid of what would happen if I did! Oh Samuel, I am so sorry! Can you ever forgive me?"

Samuel answered in a soft voice, as he realized something, "When I was overseas, I walked past a group of buildings. I heard a scream...it sounded like a woman's scream. But it didn't last long, the wind drowned it out rather quickly. Was... was... that you?"

"Yes, yes it was, Samuel. I didn't know you were there at that moment, or I would have screamed much louder. I only know I needed help. Who knows what else he would have done to me... he told me he respected women, but I had no reason to trust him. I just couldn't..."

"Shh", Samuel whispered. "We got a lot of catching up to do, it's been so long. Please, just for this moment, don't speak." Indeed, no words were spoken, none were needed, as Samuel reached up to wipe the tears from her eyes.

She reached into her pocket and pulled out the simple ring. Her hands were shaking noticeably as she passed the ring slowly from her fingers to his. Looking deep into Samuel's eyes, she whispered, "Samuel Phillips, I know that I have loved you from a distance for far too long. You always have been and always will be, my first and last love. I need to know, will you marry me, again?" Samuel whispered back, his voice shaking, "Yes, Taylor, I will marry you again, for better or worse, as long as we both shall live." He pulled her close once again, his hands sliding through her hair and he sobbed. Nothing else mattered at that moment, but the fact that he had found his bride! His princess, had returned to her prince once again, and he was never letting her go.

After a short time, she lowered her face, regretting that the moment had to end, for now. She turned slowly from Samuel to the banker, anger suddenly flaring in her eyes! She was fully prepared at that moment to expose the banker for who he is, but just as suddenly as he had shown up, Alex had left! She flew to the window, with Samuel's hand in hers. "He's gone….and taken the horses too", she replied gloomily. "We might as well bundle up here for the night; we'll leave first thing in the morning."

Chapter 14: May 6, 1930

"Quickly, we've got to get into the barn! I have a couple horses that I've been keeping for a friend of mine. He won't mind if we borrow them for a while!"

"You sure?" yelled Nathaniel, over the increasingly loud drone of the insects.

"Yeah, I'm sure; he owes me a favor anyway...." As they yanked open the door of the cellar, all three of them nearly ran down the steps in urgency! Just a few feet in front of them, the two horses, one a deep chocolate brown, named Firebolt; the other, a milky white, stood tethered to a post. Taylor pointed to the chocolate brown horse. "I'll get on this one, Nathaniel; you take the white mare...." Uh, which one is mine?" asked Samuel curiously, already guessing the answer.

"You'll be behind me on this one, of course", as a sweet smile formed on her lips.

As the hum became louder, they put their feet to the stirrups and vaulted into the saddles. Pushing their mounts for all they were worth, Samuel smiled as he looked over to see Taylor's hair flying behind her. They made their way across the landscape as another terrible sight greeted them! A massive expanse of spiders crawled steadily their way, their hairy bodies forming a slowly moving blanket along the ground! As the ecosystem had changed, insects had come out. With nothing to feed on them, the population massively grew! Breathing a short sigh of relief, they watched a huge swarm descended on the house, infesting it. Their relief suddenly turned to horror as thick, hairy bodies came their way. They seemed to even come from the trees themselves, the landscape becoming darker and more foreboding. As they tore their eyes away, they looked forward and kept heading south, until Samuel heard Taylor's voice crying out, "C'mon, I know a shortcut!" The horses wheeled around, anxious to leave this place.

Heading in a new direction, they came to an area where the land gently sloped and ended, revealing a large wooden door. With fear in her voice, Taylor explained the situation. "Ok, this door leads to an underground tunnel. My grandfather stumbled upon it many years ago, as he was one of the many people who led the slaves to freedom along the Underground Railroad. This tunnel is just a small piece of a larger network. It should lead us where we need to get to."

"And just where is that?" Samuel and Nathaniel asked, as they unmounted the horses. Taking them by the reins, they quietly opened the door, to the dark, musty tunnel.

"You'll see", said Taylor, a nervous smile playing on her lips.

Yo-Yo watched patiently as the men quickly worked to spread the oil around the wagon, but to no avail, the insects were just too ruthless. In no time at all, the swarm had descended on the wagon, the insects chewing through the wood easily and soon turning the wagon into kindling. With their wagon soon destroyed and nothing but the horse as transport, Yo-Yo looked around as he realized that he would soon be responsible for carrying one of these large, burly men. He groaned as he imagined him sagging from the weight.

One of the men spoke up, "Ok, we've lost our wagon,

but maybe it's just as well… this horse," he said, turning to Yo-Yo, "will be faster than we would have been on the wagon. There's only one horse here, so unfortunately, only one of us is gonna be ridin' him… The rest of you will be riding a wagon to our destination, should be here in 'bout an hour or so." Yo-Yo's ear perked up as one of the other men asked, "So exactly where is our destination?" "Chicago, Illinois", said the youngest man there. "If we're going to get there, we should be leaving now…."

Yo-Yo spirits fell as he heard those words. 'They were going to Chicago, Illinois'? He had heard of that as being a huge city, with large buildings and lots of shops and many, no, make that HUNDREDS of people….He dropped his head as one of the men came over to him and scratched him gently behind the ears. "It's ok, we'll figure out what we'll do once we get there. Our boss tells me that we're going there because things will be better, someday we may even become rich, leave this all behind….and who knows, there may be even something for you to do", the young man jokingly laughed. Yo-Yo hoped he was right; he'd gone this far and done everything that was asked of him, without putting up a fight. He only hoped it would mean something in the end.

Chapter 15: Evening of May 6, 1930

As Samuel, Nathaniel, and Taylor made their way cautiously into the dimly lit, twisting tunnel, they noticed a couple torches on the wall, which they quickly lit and walked slowly along the passageway. With their other hands tightly holding the reins of the horses, they slowly walked along, careful not to bump anything. After a short moment of silence, Samuel and Nathaniel whispered to Taylor, "So, uh, where does this tunnel lead us?"

Taylor turned around briefly and whispered through the silence, "It leads us directly to Chicago, Illinois, one of the historical destinations on the railroad. Now, I locked that door back there so the spiders couldn't get through; it's reinforced with metal. They'll have a time making it through there, so we should be alright. Anyways, they're probably too focused on the crops to care."

Nathaniel whispered, "Along the way, above the ground, I've been noticing rabbits and centipedes devouring the crops along the way. There seem to be too many of them to count. Won't they just find another way around, and beat us to our destination?"

"It's possible", Taylor cautioned. "But like I said, I reckon they're too worried about the crops to care. If a few of them do get through, we can handle em. Just be careful."

The longer they rode the horses, the hungrier they grew. Samuel and Nathaniel briefly stopped to rest, grabbing cheese and bread out of their knapsacks. As they ate, they looked at the surroundings curiously. Every so often, as light glinted from between cracks, spider webs could be seen shimmering in the light. Among the webs, tattered threads or pieces of rags could be seen embedded in the rocks. Samuel and Nathaniel pointed to the rags at the same time, and asked in unison, "What would those be?"

"Oh, those", stated Taylor, "Those are left over from the days of the Underground Railroad. Where you see the rags, those were quilts that the owners made to signal to the slaves. They were tied to the safe houses for the slaves, where the slaves would be hidden until it was time to move on. The way a quilt hung and even the patterns and designs sewn onto it told the slaves if the house was available or not. Since this part of the Railroad really is underground, that is where they tied the pieces of the quilts, although most of them were tied to the houses along the routes." Samuel smiled, his face reddening, impressed by Taylor's knowledge of details. After a short but satisfying lunch, they stood up and again took the reins of the white mare and Firebolt.

"How much farther do ya reckon we have to go?" Samuel finally asked on the eighth day of their journey.

"Not too much longer, about a few hours", Taylor whispered.

Very early on the final, ninth day of their long underground journey, they finally reached a worn, barely readable sign that said, **'Destination: Chicago, Illinois'**. As they made their way from the tunnel, into the bright sunlight, they looked around in wonder, as different kinds of people walked along, of different colors and builds, all of them poor and ragged. Most had their necks craned as they stared upwards. Nearly all of them were covered from head to toe in thick dust, the waves of dust from the oppressive storms coming to settle on this town, ruining what clothes they had to wear. The citizens of the town continued to stare through the haze as, hovering hundreds of feet above them, the framework of skyscrapers were dotting the horizon. The group was tempted to watch the buildings going up, but with a tug on their arms, Taylor reminded them they had somewhere they had to be. Walking quickly along the street to a fancy two-story apartment, they quickly went inside.

At the desk, a tan, average sized woman, named Marissa, turned around and in a loud, cheerful voice, bellowed, "Now, how may I help you kind people?.

"Please ma'am," Taylor spoke for the rest of the group, "We... uh... I was told you have a stateroom on the second floor. I brought a couple of... friends" At that last word; she gently squeezed Samuel's hand, as they both blushed.

"Ok, it'll be ten dollars... the woman replied. Taylor dug in her dress for the money, "... Five.... six... seven, eight, nine, and here is ten" she counted as she laid down the money.

"The stateroom is up the stairs, top floor, and two rooms are reserved, on the left side of the hallway. These days, it ain't much, but it's the very best we have."

"Thank you, ma'am," Samuel and Nathaniel both tipped their hats to her in respect, as she smiled broadly back at them, and they headed up the stairs, to their separate rooms.

As Samuel and Nathaniel set their things down slowly, they looked around the room and let out a deep sigh, "It's not much, but it'll have to do, I suppose," Samuel groaned. "It would be even better if it wasn't for all this blasted dust covering it all...." Nathaniel whispered.

Samuel spoke up suddenly, "I'm going next door to the

general store and get me something to freshen up with."

"Hold on, I'll come with ya", Nathaniel interjected.

Samuel rolled his eyes, "Ok, c'mon, no sense leaving you here to get in even more trouble" he muttered under his breath. They made their way across the street to the general store, had just completed their purchases, when Samuel laid the final item on the counter. At the same instant, it was as if a spell had come over him. He stood as still as a stone, his eyes forward, unwavering, as his brow furrowed in concentration.

"Uh, Samuel? Hello, are you there?" Nathaniel said, worried, as he waved his fingers in front of Samuel's face. "Fire", Samuel breathed the word softly. "Hope…is…a…flame.." "What in blazes are ya talking about", Nathaniel asked his friend worriedly. Shaking his head, Samuel looked down at the ground, then turned to Nathaniel and smiled. "I know why we had to come here. The Good Lord was trying to tell me something. I should have seen this much earlier! C'mon! We have work to do!"

Turning to the owner of the store, a young, pretty lady named Abby, Samuel excitedly told her, "we're gonna need fabric, lots of it, as much as you can spare. And we need some wooden stakes if you got em. Oh, and some rope.' Quickly paying for their purchases, they dashed out of the store, awkwardly carrying their bundles over to a large grassy area. "We'll set up here, Samuel told Nathaniel.

"Wait, set up, what do you mean?" Nathaniel asked, puzzled.

"No time to waste! You see those men standing over there talking? Get em over here, we're gonna need help with this!"

Nathaniel shrugged his shoulders and walked over to the men standing in a circle, talking. He wasn't in a mood to argue. He'd known Samuel at least long enough to know that when he had an idea, it had to be good, and there wasn't any way you could get him to change his mind. He explained what he knew of the situation to the men, which brought looks of concern and confusion from them. Walking back across the street, he brought Samuel over, whispering in his ear as they approached, "Now they don't fully understand what's going on, and frankly neither do I."

Samuel approached them and said, "Well, it's simple really. We need a tent. We're going to have a meeting, of sorts. Anyone that can spare anything extra can bring it, but in these difficult times, it's understandable if you can't, we won't hold it against you. I just need you strong gentlemen to pound those stakes into the ground, and ya know... make a tent." Samuel turned on his heels to face the rest of the townspeople, "I'd like to announce a meeting. Nuthin' formal, just tell your friends and neighbors and anyone that is able to come, that we got some great news we have to share with em!" The townspeople, though, reacted differently than Samuel thought they might.

Instead of them ignoring the call and going back to their own businesses, they looked around at each other, nodding in agreement. In these hard times, any good news was worth listening to. Milling around, they walked up to their friends, family members, and even people they hadn't even met and asked them to come to this unique meeting. Within an hour, after the tent had been set up and all the townspeople, hundreds in all, had gathered in a large group.

Kyle Nathan Buller

Samuel made his way to the front of the tent and in a bellowing voice, spoke even louder than he thought he was capable of. "Hello ladies and gentlemen,", he said. "You may wonder why I've called you here. I had a vision, and I have some very important news to share. It's gonna be the best news you've ever heard. But, before I begin, I urge you to not forget it. I bring you fantastic, incredible news that is for all of you!" He humbly introduced to them the story of a man who, like them, was born into this world and never had a warm place to lay his head. This man knew what they were going through in their lives, because like them, he knew what it meant to be lonely, poor, forgotten, and abused. As he continued the story of the man who was born of a virgin and led a sinless life, yet faced temptations like the rest of us, more and more people came forth, most of them just sitting or reclining on the cold ground. As he continued the story of the birth, life, death and resurrection of this man, Samuel smiled broadly as even more came forth to hear the message.

Samuel then said something very important, "I remember one terrible day, I lost my only friend. It was a very beautiful, very loyal horse. I lived on a small farm and didn't have much. My wife, I thought, had died." Next, Samuel motioned to Cassidy. She ran up next to him, her eyes moist with tears. He slipped his rough hand around her waist and pulled her close. "I was angry at God for taking her away. While on a trip to visit family overseas, I was knocked unconscious by a cruel man, while she was kidnapped, and when I came to, a letter lay beside me, telling me that she had died from a disease. For years, I believed that that was the truth. Then later, I discovered I had been lied to again. That wound cut me so deeply. I didn't show it on the outside, but inwardly, my heart wanted revenge. I didn't know what I would do if I ever came face to face with the one responsible.

Years later, I found out that was only the first of many wrongs that I would have to endure. The same man, I later found out, who was responsible for that betrayal, would come for my horse. That man took him from me and I was left with nothing. All I could rely on was God. I was an empty, broken person and I became angry at the One who had created me. I became desperate and did things I am not proud of. I had accepted Christ at a young age, and am a believer. In my anguish, I thought getting him back would satisfy me. But along my journey, I have learned that anger with God is only a good thing when it causes you to draw closer to Him. Being alone and doing things your own way is not what God wants. He needs us to have relationship with Him and with other believers. You see, I was teased as a child for my faith. Children thought my faith was a fairy tale! But, looking back, I do suppose believing in God is much like a fairy tale."

An older woman in the back row stood up, her face crinkled in thought, "What are you talking about?" she asked. Samuel looked at her and said, "I am glad you asked me that question. Let's think about it this way. When we accept Christ, we are adopted into his kingdom, his realm. We are made royalty, sons and daughters of the King of Kings. From then on, it is our appointed mission to stand up for the truth and believe in His word. We encounter enemies of the King, wherever we go. But instead of fighting with them, it is our job to do our best to bring them into His light, putting on the armor of God. His greatest commandment is to love our neighbor. When we encounter allies in our quest, that fact alone, the we do have friends to stand with us and encourage us, should give us great joy! The only enemy we have to actively fight against is Satan himself. All other people who reject the ways of God, they are simply tools of that old serpent. But Christians must stand up for the truth of God, and if that means that people must be humbled in order for Him and His ways to be exalted, then so be it! Christians need to understand who their fight is really against! Not flesh and blood, but against invisible forces. In the book of Revelation, Satan is described as a dragon. Every fairy tale does indeed need a dragon, or at the very least, a powerful villain. But we don't have to fight the dragon alone! God has given every believer His spirit and power to fight evil. The outcome has already been foretold since before time began. The line in the sand was drawn the day Adam and Even sinned, and the battle cry was sounded the day the Lord died on the cross. A great man once said, "Fairy tales exist not so children can know that dragons exist, children already know that. Fairy tales exist so that children can know that dragons can be defeated."

Samuel nodded to the woman, "Thank you for the question." Anyway, that single event of being teased as a child, made me not want to share my faith with people. I figured they would make fun of me just like I was made fun of. But I have discovered that God places people in your path to draw you closer to Him. I believe those bullies, in some way, put me on the path to being a farmer and meeting my dear horse. I also believe that He brought me to this place in time, and through the storms I went through, so that I could give others hope for the future. I believe He has brought me here, in this place, so that I could minister to you, showing you what I've gone through. Maybe I could help you in some small way, with what life throws at you. I am going to try to honor God and rain down grace and mercy on you, as He has done with me. I pray that He continues to help me to do well."

In a booming voice, Samuel continued his message, "I realize that none of us have much or may not even have anything at all. But when you come to the cross, you don't need to bring anything. All He asks is that you come with humility and sincerity. You don't need riches, you don't need to know everything, and He just needs you to come. His greatest, deepest desire is to have a relationship with us humans, flawed as we are. Two thousand years ago, he died a horrible, violent death to prove how deep His love for us goes. A young boy, not much older than seven, asked, "But you said before that he was a human, so did he stay dead?"

In a joyful voice, Samuel screamed, a smile widening on his face, "No, that is how amazing His love is! Jesus showed his power by rising from the dead after three days in a borrowed tomb! He was completely God and completely man! You see? Just like we have to borrow each other's belongings because we don't have the money to go out and buy what we would like to, Jesus spent three days in a tomb that wasn't even his! He had everything that He could possibly want at his command. But he cast it all aside so he could come down to this dirty, filthy, sinful world, and die to have a relationship with us! He's walked the same paths we have, been in the same situations! He knows our pain and our loss! He's felt it too! And when our lives seem like a dead end, Jesus can come in and open up new doors! We just have to be willing to lay down our pride and trust Him!

There is not one person so damaged, so evil, that God cannot reach him! No one is beyond God's grace, mercy and forgiveness! He isn't willing that anyone should be sent to hell! That is why he came, to die for the sins of everyone, no matter how horrible they are. It comes down to our own decisions. Who will you give your allegiance to? All I know for certain is that me and Taylor, we shall serve the Lord with our dying breath."

The ground was so crowded and filled with people, the rest of them had no choice but to climb trees and sit in the branches, listening to the speaker. As Samuel told more and more of the story, the people listened intently, most of their eyes filling with tears. They were coming to realize that this wasn't just a story after all. This was real! More real than anything they had ever known! The sinless God had become man and come to this earth to identify with their needs and their brokenness! "Long ago, I was helping a man I had never met; I rescued his calf during one of the fiercest dust storms we've had. I promised myself I wouldn't stop until the animal was safe, even though I was heartbroken after selling my horse. Don't you see? Christ Himself is heartbroken over our sin! It killed him, literally, to see our hearts so blackened and evil! But He never stops giving us chances every single day! Every day you wake up is another possibility to start again! Be grateful for what you have!"

Samuel spoke with raw power, his hunger for the Word, nearly relentless, "Those grasshopper plagues and dust storm we have all endured, they are similar to the storms of life we all face. The important thing is to praise God through the storm! Learn to dance in the rain, even when things are going terrible, give the Master glory!"

"I learned to trust in God through everything, even during the darkest moments. A man, whom I had grown to trust, betrayed me. We worked together, doing the same thing the Good Lord is allowing me to do for you now, telling others about Jesus. He became jealous, and he took everything I had from me, but he could never destroy my faith! But even during those times, I clung to the words of Christ, the one who is a friend of sinners, who is hope for the hopeless, and rest for the weary! We may be poor in material things, even poor in spirit, but I've learned that if you have Christ as your foundation, and people around you who are willing to lift you up and help you through life, you are wealthy beyond imagination."

Just then, Samuel reached over, grabbing a small loaf of bread. Holding it aloft, he said, "This represents our Savior's body, broken for us, so that we may live in His presence forever. Take this, eat, and remember His sacrifice." He passed the loaf of bread to a young boy, who in turn passed to someone else, and soon everyone had broken off a piece, eating it. He then went over to where a large bowl of water lay on the ground. He took it and appointed a handful of the men to pass out metal cups. Each person was given water and when all had been served, he said in a loud voice, "This represents the blood of Christ's sacrifice, poured in love for us all."

"Shouldn't it be red, the color of Jesus' blood?" a young girl answered innocently.

"What is your name, little one?" Samuel asked her with a wide smile on his face.

"It's Emily, sir", she answered nervously. She motioned over to a young boy with glasses, a book in his hands, as he smiled in wonder, "and this here's my brother, Max."

"Emily is right", Samuel spoke to the crowd. "Jesus' blood was spilled out for us, and red is the color of that blood. But since we can't afford wine, we use water, to signify the cleansing blood, as well as the water of life, that He is to us all now! Drink of this cup and remember His sacrifice. Thank you for coming, Emily and Max. You may go back to your parents and sit down." After they had all taken of the water and the bread, the service continued.

As Samuel lowered his voice, he sat back down, his head bowed. Just then, a deep hum began somewhere in the crowd, gaining strength until it became a clear note. A little black girl in the audience, with braids in her hair, began singing alone. Her voice lifting up to heaven, the rest of the audience soon followed along in a joyful song of worship and praise:

O Lord My God
When I in awesome wonder
Consider all the worlds thy hands have made
I see the stars, I hear the rolling thunder
Thy power throughout the universe displayed,
Then sings my soul, my Savior God to Thee
How Great Thou Art, How Great Thou Art!
When through the woods and forest glades I wander
And hear the birds sing sweetly in the trees
When I look down from lofty mountain grandeur
And hear the brook and feel the gentle breeze
Then sings my soul, my Savior God to Thee
How Great Thou Art, How Great Thou Art!
Then sings my soul, my Savior God to Thee
How Great Thou Art, How Great Thou Art!
I think of God, His son not sparing
Sent Him to die, I scarce can take it in
But on that cross, my burden gladly bearing
He bled and died to take away my sin
Then sings my soul, How Great Thou Art!
When Christ shall come with shouts of acclamation

And take me home, what joy shall fill my heart!
Then I shall bow in humble adoration
And there proclaim, My God How Great Thou Art!
Then sings my soul, my Savior God to Thee,
How Great Thou Art, How Great Thou Art!

As the music slowly faded, Samuel leaned over to the girl, and placed a soft hand on her shoulder. With tears in his eyes, said, "Thank you, Taia." A profound hush had settled over the crowd and no one spoke or even whispered. Bowing their heads and closing their eyes, they unashamedly thanked their Creator for His boundless love. After another hour of speaking, Samuel finished his message, which wasn't really his message at all. Afterwards, he answered questions from some of the children, the townspeople forming a line. Each of them shook his hand, thanking him, their eyes wet with tears. At the end of the service, as the line neared its end, Samuel gave an altar call, inviting anyone to accept Christ. Many of the townspeople answered the call and accepted the teachings and sacrificial love of Jesus Christ of Nazareth, and many lives were changed as a result. Immediately following the service, a group of the men got together instruments, playing jazz and gospel music to celebrate the miracles.

In the midst of a conversation with a young boy, Samuel looked up briefly, his eyes drawn to a figure walking away quickly from the tent. The figure turned slowly, crouched down among the shadows of the buildings, as if trying to stay hidden, and entered the hotel. "That's odd", thought Samuel, "I wonder why he's being so secretive." But he went back to greeting the remainder of the townspeople, not giving it a second thought. After they had all left, some of the men stayed to help him tear down the tent. After it had all been cleaned up, Samuel shook hands with the men, talking with them a while about what they had heard. With smiles on their faces, they made their way back to the bread lines, as it was nearly dinnertime. Samuel turned and walked back to the hotel, whispering a prayer of thanks to God for all the miracles that had been performed this day.

Samuel walked into the hotel, up the steps, past Taylor's room. He raised his hand to the door and almost knocked, but hesitated, he wasn't sure why. Lowering his hand, he simply put his face close to the door and whispered in a soft voice, breaking with emotion, "Taylor, if you're there, there's something you must know, something I need to tell you before it's too late. I fear that it soon will be. I should have told you this long ago in the farmhouse, but, I...I...love...you." Those fateful words poured forth from him in a gush of emotion. In embarrassment, he turned toward his room and opened the door, totally exhausted. As his door closed, at the same moment, across the hall, a faint, shallow voice whispered through tears of incredible joy, "Samuel... I love you too, and, thank you. You'll never know what you've done, for me, and all of us."

As Samuel lay on his bed, his eyes closed, a soft knock came at the door. He slowly got up and opened it, expecting to see Taylor, but instead found a young boy. Kneeling down, Samuel asked the boy, "What is it?" "Please sir... I just wanted to ask a favor of you." In his hand he held a yo-yo. "Would you please take good care of this for me? I wanted to go play with some friends, but I'm afraid it will get lost if I hold onto it. My parents said it was ok if I go. I know what you did for us, and it sounds crazy sayin' this to a stranger, but I feel as if I can trust you." Samuel replied, "Ok, I will hold onto it for you as long as you need." Samuel gave the boy a warm smile and ruffled his hair, as the boy went off to play with his friends. He smiled to himself as he pocketed the toy. Closing the door, he got up in bed, turned off the light and fell asleep soon after his head hit the pillow, totally forgetting about the yo-yo, as he fell into a relaxing slumber.

Shortly after the events of the revival, following a well-deserved nap, Taylor stood up, refreshed, looking in awe around her room. It was adorned with the finest things that could be afforded in that time, somewhat plain, but no less beautiful. She never thought she would ever see anything so nice. In her eyes, it was all so beautiful. As she turned the corner to go wash her hands and freshen up, she reached out to turn on the light switch, fumbling in the dark. The instant the light switch came on; she heard a loud buzzing sound as smoke came from the outlet. The next instant, smoke trailed up as sparks came shooting up as well. Turning to run from the room, she briefly noticed flames starting to spread from the light fixture, as it landed to the floor with a loud crash, quickly engulfing the entire room in thick flames and rolling, billowing smoke!

Chapter 16: May 15, 1930

Yo-Yo and one of the young men, who had begrudgingly been picked to ride on his back toward the city, were about to set off, when another young man, spoke up. "I vote for leaving as soon as we can, we are about fifty miles from the city. If we leave now, we can make it easily by nightfall. The other men agreed wholeheartedly, but Yo-Yo had a nagging feeling that something just wasn't quite right. Suddenly, without warning, Yo-Yo thrashed his head aside, rearing up on his back legs, as the grip of the man holding his reins loosened! The horrible feeling he was having becoming stronger! He knew his friend was alive, and needed him! As he galloped away from the men, he felt the wind whipping through his mane as his saddle dropped to the ground, rolling into a ravine.

The men cursed and screamed at him to come back, throwing their hats to the ground in anger, but by then he was too far away to hear anything they said. The dry fields and parched ground became a blur as he ran as fast as his little hooves could possibly carry him. He had friends who had run so fast they fell over from exhaustion, but this was different. No one knew Samuel the way he did, and at that moment, nothing meant more than being there for his friend. He sped across the landscape faster than he ever had; all the while remembering his father, winning all those races, years ago.

As he ran breathlessly along the ground, his hooves pounding, he passed a section of nearly abandoned farmhouses, as a group of children stood sadly on the property. With tears running down their little faces, they slowly broke into huge smiles as they saw this horse galloping past them. The young boys stood in their ragged garments and waved their hands around wildly, the little girls also screaming excitedly, as this young horse provided a moment of inspiration for these children, in the middle of uncertainty.

This feeling of elation and pride gave Yo-Yo an extra burst of speed as he breathed through his nose in short, ragged gasps. He had no idea how long he had been running, as he could no longer hear the cries of the men, only the cheers of the children as more youngsters gathered beside him, encouraging him on. As the cheers grew louder and louder, he nearly missed what he was searching for. A large wooden sign on the right side of a barely noticeable trail said, **Chicago - 3 Miles**. The bond between him and his friend grew stronger, warning him expectantly. He just knew that was where his friend was! It had to be true!

Quickly turning the corner, he sped on for his destination, not yet knowing what waited for him once he got there. Within half an hour, he had entered the outskirts of the bustling city, and what a sight it was! Muscular men in trench coats and fedoras were walking solemnly along the streets, a hush had settling over the city as thick mounds of dust from the storms had settled everywhere, on every storefront, every tree, even the roads were burdened with a thick layer of it. Yo-Yo's sensitive nose sniffed the air, taking in the scents of the city; the stale scent of dust, the scent of the various people walking up and down the streets, and yet another scent he couldn't quite place….A thick, musty or smoky odor… Yo-Yo turned abruptly as a man yelled, "Fire!"

Turning his head, Yo-Yo whinnied in horror as a thick plume of smoke billowed up from a building to his right, the flames dancing high into the evening. The man, who had yelled the warning, spoke again, his voice hoarse.... "We need a large tub, deep enough for a lot of water....those flames reach pretty high, it's gonna take a while to put em out." The middle-aged man stared out at the crowd, as his eyes scanned the groups of people.

He froze as his eyes settled on Yo-Yo, "I don't know where you came from, but you seemed to arrive just in the nick of time. We're gonna need you, my friend...." he spoke gently, walking over to the frightened animal. As the men took his reins, Yo-Yo reared back but slowly quieted as he remembered some advice his master had told him many years ago, 'Being a man means facing whatever comes your way with bravery."

Letting out a small snort, he allowed himself to be led to a small brick building. "Now, stay right there", said the man, his blue eyes staring at Yo-Yo very kindly. Running into the building, the man in charge yelled orders to his fellow workers around him as they struggled to pull a cart with a large box set in place atop it, propelled by wheels, a chimney sticking up from the middle of it. Yo-Yo breathed softly as a couple of the men came in front of him, fastening a harness to his face. To this harness, they attached the reins, the flames leaping higher as they worked urgently.

With two of the burlier men pulling the wagon behind him, they hitched it to him and he groaned wearily as he felt a man hastily mount his back. His ears perked up though, as he heard two of the men talking, "Now, you're gonna take this here bucket of water and we're all gonna form a line, passing the bucket from one man to the next. Yo-Yo here is gonna be hauling this steam engine...."

One of the other men quickly interrupted, "Wait... aren't we gonna use those new... oh, whaddya call em..... internal combustion engines...?

"We would have", said the younger man, "but they have to be shipped from Pennsylvania. Workers there, well they ain't faring the best....so that shipment's been delayed. We were supposed to have horses do all the work, but with the state of the economy, none have been able to volunteer. Well, I reckon what I'm trying to say is that this horse is fixin' to be the first horse to ever do anything like this. So, I guess our new friend here," he clapped Yo-Yo on the back, "is gonna get us outta this mess." Yo-Yo nervously looked from the men to the fire and back again. He only hoped he could do what it took to get the job done.

With all the volunteers scrambling to quickly get into place, Yo-Yo and Firebolt were in the front of the pack, the men behind him with wooden buckets, passing water back and forth between them. A meager line formed as they retrieved water from a large basin, their hearts soon sinking, realizing that the flames were getting higher with each bucket of water they poured. What they were doing wasn't enough, they needed more volunteers, a larger source of water, in short, they needed more help than they could get on their own. "Heave, ho!" the men struggled to dump the water on the fire, but to no avail. After an hour of struggling, they were about to slow down, when they heard thin, weak voices coming from the building!

"Please, someone help us...can't last... much longer!" a group of voices, uttered desperately. The men doubled their efforts as they worked quickly to douse the fire. The man in front yelled at his partners, "You two are gonna have to go in after em, we're trying to do all we can out here, but we need a rescue unit, we got two, maybe three people trapped in there!"

With the men continuously struggling to dump the water on the burning hotel, the remaining helpers stripped to their underwear, running in blindly to find the trapped survivors. With their hands shielding their faces, they squinted as the heat seared their skin. "If you're close by, give us some kind of a sign..." they screamed above the crackle of the flames.

"Yes, we're right here... this way... to....your....left.....please hurry!" Taylor screamed as a couple of weak voices cried as well, a pile of timbers tumbling down in front of them, nearly hiding the survivors.

The rescuers proceeded cautiously as they made their way to the source of the voices. They stopped abruptly, amid the flames, as a large timber dropped from the ceiling, very nearly crushing them! Through the thick flames and smoke, they could barely make out the shapes of three individuals huddled on the floor, below the smoke, all three of them holding hands. As they came close enough to get a hold of them, the younger man reached out to grab what he thought was Samuel's arm when he slipped on the pile of debris and started to fall. At the last instant, just as it seemed he would perish in the flames, the young man caught Samuel's arm as Samuel used his final bit of strength he had in that moment, pulling him to safety. The young man retreated back the way he had came, as the heat became too much for him. His face grew sad and sorrowful as he mouthed the words, *I'm sorry*, a thick plume of smoke totally covering him as he left. Samuel let out a scream of frustration, breathing heavily from the exertion as he, Taylor and Nathaniel still huddled under the smoke. But soon, they got to their feet, holding hands as they made their way slowly across to their rescuers.

Samuel used his arm to shield his face from the heat, his hands squeezing Taylor's tighter, as she squeezed Nathaniel's tighter in return. Peering a short distance through the flames, he said, "Just ahead, see those timbers? We'll have to make our way up them and across to safety." *Whoosh!* From a room to their right, a huge jet of flame, came flinging out of the doorway, blocking their progress. They quickly turned around, their eyes searching frantically for another way. Ahead of them, another set of timbers lay at an angle across the fiery expanse, bridging the gap from one floor to the next. They turned and shielded their faces from the terrible heat, as they ran back the way they had come. Taylor turned to Samuel, fear creeping into her voice, "I...I can't do this! Samuel, I'm scared...What if it doesn't hold?" Samuel turned to look at her, his face caked with sweat. "Yes, you can. I believe in you. You've been through much more than this. *We've* been through much more than this. I won't let you go, I promise!" Taylor looked in Samuel's eyes and saw only pure trust and faith there. She took a deep breath and whispered, "Ok, for you. I'm still scared to death. But I'll do this." She turned back and slowly kneeling down, she placed her hands on the creaky, wooden ramp, making her way up very slowly.

"Just don't look down, and whatever you do, try not to get caught on anything!", Samuel ordered. Along the length of the boards, an old rope wormed its way up to the second floor. It was attached to a metal claw and, as the building became unstable and caved in, had become wrapped around a decrepit wooden post. The floor that supported the post sharply sloped downward, threatening to fall. Samuel quickly wondered why the rope would be there in the first place. 'It must have been put there for rescue purposes. Maybe it got wrapped around the post during the fire, and the floor fell under the weight of the debris.' Samuel thought to himself. Taylor leaned forward wrapping her arms tight around the boards. She scooted her body upwards, squeezing her eyes tight. Suddenly the boards creaked, and she screamed as her body dropped a couple feet, then came to an abrupt standstill! "It's ok! Just keep coming!", Samuel yelled. "I can't do it!", she protested. He made his way past her and gingerly stepped across the boards, until he was facing her. Kneeling down slowly, he whispered, "We can't go back down to the first floor! That way is blocked, we'll never get through! Taylor, I need you to look into my eyes! Don't focus on anything else! I promised not to let anything happen to you, and I intend on keepin' that promise, no matter what!" Taylor nodded slowly, her body trembling as she scooted up the ramp slowly, one inch at a time.

Holding out his hand as she came within reach, Samuel said, "Ok, now just grab on tight, and don't let go!" No sooner had she reached out her hand, then the boards snapped in two under her, sending her plummeting down! Letting out a terrible scream, Taylor flailed her arms desperately. Samuel's heart sunk as she fell to the flames below! At the last possible instant, her fingers wrapped around the very bottom of the frayed, weakened rope! "Samuel, help me!", Taylor begged, as she swayed back and forth helplessly, the heat of the flames washing over her. Her hands turned white from the strain as she held fast to the rope. "You gotta climb! I can't reach you here!", Samuel pleaded. Taylor's hands shook as she pulled herself very slowly up the rope. The metal claw dug into the wood tight as she made her way up very slowly. Her palms sweating, and her muscles straining, she pulled herself up the rest of the way. Samuel swung the rope slowly over to him, as he reached down and grabbed her, pulling her up. Breathing heavily, Samuel laid her gently on a sturdy patch of the floor. With a start, she involuntarily leaped out of the way, shrieking as a weak section of floor behind her gave way, tumbling down into the flames! Jumping into the arms of her rescuer, she nearly toppling him over as she held tight to Samuel. He pulled back and looked into her eyes, brushing the hair from her blackened face as he whispered, "Now see, that wasn't so bad, was it?"

Taylor smiled playfully, pushed against his chest, catching him before he started to lose his balance, and gratefully kissed him. They slowly walked along the length of the floor, occasionally stopping as weak sections gave way. Soon, they all started coughing as the smoke found its way into their lungs. Samuel wrapped his one arm around Taylor's waist, his other arm around Nathaniel's shoulder. Walking faster, they stared straight ahead as their eyes watered from the smoke and flames. Though their vision was blurry, they could see just ahead, a glass window with a small, jagged opening, the light of day streaming through it! "Come on! We're almost there!", Samuel urged. They continued to run as they heard the crackle of flames and the creaking of weak timbers behind them!

On the ground, one of the men heard the sounds of Taylor, Samuel, and Nathaniel on the floor above him gradually get louder and louder! As his heart began pounding, he knew what they had to do. He screamed to a woman beside him, "We need a large blanket now!" She ran next door and soon had returned with a rather large quilt, yelling above the roar of the flames, "This belonged to my daughter. She passed away two months ago." In respect, the man placed a hand on her shoulder and smiled. Then he threw it to some of the other men fighting the fire, "We need a few of you to hold this out tight! Stretch it out! We got those people that are trapped, they are on the second floor, and they're about to jump!" Quickly the men stretched out the blanket to catch the trapped survivors. The leader of this band of brave souls, the one who had heard the survivors, stood directly in front of the hotel, his eyes fixed on the window, "Please God, I beg of You, let this work!"

    Samuel dropped his shoulder and threw his weight against the window as glass shattered! Stepping back a short distance, he turned to Nathaniel and said "You gotta jump, and whatever happens, it's been a pleasure knowing you my friend." Nathaniel answered his comrade, "Remember when you helped me search for my calf, and you didn't stop till we found him? I realize you easily could have, the storm was so awful... and you told me not to give up, that we would find him. Now it's time you take your own advice. We'll be ok. This isn't the final scene, my friend. He took Taylor's hand as they prepared to jump. "Don't worry, whatever happens, I will care for her. I won't let you down." Nathaniel and Cassidy jumped as shards of glass bit into their skin. As they fell, above them, the top floor of the hotel exploded in a ball of fire, sending debris raining down on them! The rescuers down below pulled the blanket as tight as they could. They felt it nearly ripping from the strain as Cassidy and Nathaniel fell. Screaming, the survivors both landed with a thud against the blankets.

Breathing heavily, they stood up slowly, coughing as black smoke covered their faces. Using one hand to steady themselves, they drew in deep breaths of fresh, clean air as they blinked their watery eyes. As their vision cleared, Taylor and Nathaniel looked around them, grateful for the help. Nathaniel gasped in horror as he realized his worst fears, "Where is Samuel?" Taylor looked back at him, then her gaze wandered as her eyes kept searching helplessly, "He's not here!" she screamed. One of the men looked at her grimly and said, "Samuel was talking with a young boy who had a yo-yo in his hand. I overheard him promise to keep it safe. He must have dropped it, chances are he went in after it. I'm sorry, there's nothing we can do now..." She ran to go back in the burning building, but rough, thick arms, wrapped around her, holding her back. Her mouth opened in a wordless scream as she struggled, "No! Please! I have to go back! He's my husband!"

"Please ma'am, wait here.", one of the men ordered, as he stepped in her line of sight. "We'll send someone in to find him. It's unsafe for you." Taylor gritted her teeth and glared at the man speaking to her, "No, I'll go. It's my duty as his *wife!* I told him 'till death do us part, and I *meant* it! Now, please be so kind and let... me... go!" She stopped short as a tall, but lanky man off to the side, raised his hand. His voice was clear and very direct as he showed no fear,"No I'll go, please, send me." One of the men fighting the fire said to him, "You can't risk it! We won't let you! You'll die in there! You can't go!" The man interrupted him quickly, pointing a finger his direction, "Now I want you to listen to me good. If something needs to be done, I wanna be the one to do it. Samuel told us, 'No greater love has any man than he lay down his life for his friends. After that revival meetin' we had, all of these people," he spread his arms wide to encompass the multitude, "are my friends. Many of em, I don't even know, but I figure that we share a bond now, and I'd do whatever it takes to save the lot of 'em, even give my own life. It may sound foolish to you, but it makes all the sense in the world to me." As he backpedaled into the building, he said more confidently. "Now stay here! Don't come in after me! God willin' I'll be back! And if the Good Lord ain't willin', well, that's for Him to decide." That last statement, he spoke with such peace and confidence, as a huge smile broke across his face.

    No one barely had time to protest as the fellow ran in the building without another word, the towering flames and deep darkness swallowed him whole, as the men outside just stared in awe. Tears fell down Taylor's face as she realized the sacrifice he was about to make. One of the men at the front of the line spoke quietly and reverently, "He's got courage, that one does. I reckon we all should look at our fellow man the same way." The minutes passed by very slowly as they all waited patiently, holding their breath for any sign of either man. As the time marched on, the seconds gradually ticking away, their spirits began to slowly but surely sink. The opportunity for either of them to make it out alive was slowly beginning to pass by...

Chapter 17: Late Afternoon on May 15, 1930

As the men outside the fire hopelessly tried to douse the encroaching flames with their meager supply of water and dwindling line of manpower, Yo-Yo looked down hopelessly. In his mind it appeared as if a large empty chasm opened before him, like a runner whose finish line was replaced by a brick wall; almost as if everything they had worked for would just simply end right here.... Suddenly, a large crowd of voices joined the men, more voices than they had heard in a very long time. A large commotion could be heard as Yo-Yo looked around in wonder, hardly believing what he saw! It seemed as if the entire town had joined to help them.

Everywhere he looked, men, women and children, were aiding their cause! As far as the eye could see, buckets were passed down the line, from one person to the next, and as soon as they came to Yo-Yo, they were nearly as full as they had began with! With so many people rushing to help them, the fire was extinguished in a short time, with the rescue fully complete!

Some of the women ran inside their houses and took warm blankets, draping them over the survivors; then they were led to a makeshift hospital a block away. Yo-Yo looked around and was overwhelmed at the amazing display of help that came seemingly out of nowhere! He didn't understand, but he was grateful nevertheless.

As minutes slowly trudged along into hours, the survivors were finally released from the hospital. Taylor and Nathaniel came out slowly, on weak legs, coughing and hacking, as black soot covered them from head to toe. As they waited patiently for the final survivor, an unexplained feeling of dread came over Yo-Yo, similar to the fright he felt the day he was sold.

Suddenly, a thin, tiny, weak figure stumbled from the building. His hair was in disarray as; he too, was covered in black soot, his clothes nearly torn to shreds. He was coughing and hacking much worse than the other two though, his chest heaving hard through what was left of his shirt. A mass of humanity huddled around him. He looked around him slowly, as if searching for someone. "Where is he?", Samuel wheezed. "Where is who?", one of the men asked. "The man who rescued me. He was just a tall, thin fellow, he couldn't have survived all the smoke. He pointed to the way out, and then, the smoke, the flames, they just..." His back against a tree, he slid to the ground as the realization suddenly hit him. He wiped away tears as he said thoughtfully, "He risked his life to save mine..." Lowering his head, he thanked God for people willing to sacrifice their lives for others. As he let out a thick cough, he raised his head, fixing his eyes on a peculiar, but familiar animal far in the distance...

'I.... can't believe this...... it can't be...' Samuel whispered as he raised himself to his feet, stumbling closer in an attempt to get a better look. As his eyes slowly came into focus, he lifted his thin hands to his mouth, his fingers shaking violently. As a wordless scream escaped his lips, thick, giant tears ran unbidden down his wrinkled cheeks.

The citizens of the town had formed a large semicircle around the survivors, staring curiously as this old farmer, obviously shaken up by events which they could not yet understand. As Samuel's legs slowly wobbled toward Yo-Yo, he closed his eyes against the fierce onslaught of emotion, and balled his hands into tight fists, barely able to regain composure. He ran as fast and hard as his weak legs could carry him, his breath coming shallow as his heart hammered in his chest! Samuel pulled up sharply, feeling a hand press tightly against his shoulder, within a foot of his dear, loyal friend. A squeak escaped his lips as he whispered, "I... I thought you were lost... or dead..."

At the sound of that final word, his shoulders shook and he bawled louder than he had in a very, very long time. Part of him felt foolish for crying in the midst of all these people, but he didn't care anymore. His friend had come back to him, and in that moment, he knew that no matter what came their way, everything was going to be all right. As his legs became weak from the overpowering emotion, he collapsed in the dirt and ashes of the aftermath of the fire. The hotel was charred and blackened, a complete loss, but thankfully, no one had perished so far.

Yo-Yo nearly ran toward his master, a look of compassion and overwhelming love on his face. Giant horse tears began streaming down his face as well, but now sorrow had been replaced with incredible joy! Licking Samuel's face, he lowered his head and stepped into Samuel, letting his master wrap his hands around him.

"Yo-Yo, I'm so sorry, I should have come looking for you....please forgive me..."

As if in answer, Yo-Yo's nose prodded against Samuel's chin, as he stuck his tongue out, slowly licking the face of his master once again Thick gnarled fingers grasped Yo-Yo's mane as he bent his legs and bowed closer to the ground, letting Samuel nuzzle against him, his warm hands stroking his back and shoulders gently as he was gripped tightly in a protective embrace. Yo-Yo slowly closed his eyes in contentment and neighed softly as his master, once again reunited with his long lost friend, comforted him.

As the time slowly crept on, Yo-Yo realized he had fallen asleep. Blinking his eyes, he looked around him and understood, with a start, that he was no longer able to feel Samuel's embrace around him. Swishing his tail, he craned his neck to look around him. An unusual hush had settled over the crowd. Most of the people in the crowd had tears in their eyes; some of them turned away, so as not to be seen. As handkerchiefs dabbed their eyes, he got his legs under him and just as he was about to stand up, he felt a sickening thud beside him. As he turned his head again slowly, part of him not wanting to know what had made the thud, he neighed loudly as his heart broke for the second time, much worse than it had broken the first. A figure slid down off Yo-Yo, now lying on its side in the dust and ashes, its head resting against its arm. The thud he had abruptly heard as he stood up was the sound of his master, sliding off his body, now lying on the ground, unmoving.

A terrible, lonely sadness overtook Yo-Yo as he nudged Samuel's lifeless body with his snout, over and over again, begging him to come back. Taylor slowly walked to the front of the crowd, her eyes welling with tears as she dabbed them away with her fingers... "I am so, very, very sorry... The smoke and dust and everything were just too much for him to handle...." "She wrapped her arms around Yo-Yo's neck and just wept, her body shaking.

As he stepped closer to his master's wife, she softly mumbled against him, "He's gone... but he loved you... He loved us all, so very, very much...we know that." Yo-

Yo was unable to speak, but inside, all sorts of unanswered questions were bubbling to the surface of his mind.... "Why? What had he done to deserve this? Where would he go now? Why had he come this far, just to have this happen? Where was God during all this? It was all so very unfair..."

As if in answer to all his questioning, a figure slowly sauntered to the front of the crowd. Yo-Yo looked around him and noticed that everyone else in the crowd, had become still as stones. 'Was this a dream?' he wondered. Staring into the warm, peaceful eyes of the stranger, he recognized at once the straw hat and the long mustache. He was also carrying the same wooden staff he had on that day, so long ago it seemed.

"Hello, my four legged friend... I know it has been a long time, but I am here with a message to ease your sorrow. Although I don't have the answer to why your friend had to pass from this life, I can assure you, he is in a much better place. You have done nothing to deserve this; death is part of the natural cycle of life. He loved you more completely than you can imagine, he would have done anything for you. I do not know where your travels will take you from here, but there is One who does know... and I can promise you, He has been with you every step of your journey. He has never left and He never will."

Yo-Yo turned his head and cocked his ears, staring at this strange man. As he blinked away tears, he was again strangely comforted by the man's words. "And I do have one final message for you, my friend." With these words, the figure stooped and took a circular wooden toy, charred by the smoke and flames, from the lifeless fingers of Yo-Yo's master. As he unwound the toy and unfurled the string, he looped the end of it in his fingers and grabbed the wooden part of the toy in his warm hand "This, my friend, is a new toy, that just a couple decades ago, has been invented, known as a yo-yo..." Yo-Yo's eyes widened, the man replying as if reading his thoughts, "Yes, just like your namesake. Samuel wanted you to have that name because it meant something to him, something special and unique.

Samuel had this in his hand, once the fire started. It belonged to a young boy whose father was a policeman, years ago. His father was crippled while trying to take down a criminal. This boy was crippled as well, but by polio, as Samuel used to be. This yo-yo was the only thing the poor boy had to keep him busy. And it did indeed teach him something new. The boy gave it to him before the fire, to keep it safe. He wanted to play with some friends, so he struck up a conversation with Samuel. Your master agreed to keep it so it wouldn't get lost. Well, he must have forgot he was carrying it, once the fire started, and then he was caught up in the fire. When he went in the first time, he nearly escaped with his life, but in all the confusion, he dropped it again. He knew he would never forgive himself if he didn't go back to rescue it, and return it to its rightful owner. Samuel bravely risked his life to rescue it and return it to the boy."

"You see," he said as he quickly snapped his wrist downward, with his fingers to the ground. His voice became soft and slow, "all of us upon this earth, are like this yo-yo...when we are born, The Good Shepherd brings us to this earth as innocent babes," With that, he let the toy fall to the ground, still tethered to the string. "And this string is like His spirit, given to us when we believe in The Good Shepherd, so that we may stay connected to

Him. In the Good Book, it says that nothing can pull us from His hand, If, and only if, we stay connected to the string of His grace and mercy, we will always return to the palm of His loving hand." To illustrate this last point, he turned his wrist again so that his fingers were facing the ground, the toy rolling up against the string, coming to rest safely in his hand. "It is possible, very possible in fact, if we aren't careful, to stray from His path." He showed this by flicking his wrist continuously, the yo-yo bouncing back and forth faster than Yo-Yo could concentrate. He then passed the string back and forth between his fingers and, Yo-Yo looked up as the wooden circular part of the yo-yo flew off the string. The man craned his neck upward, concentrating hard as he watched it fall back on the string, totally secure once again. With a few more flicks of his wrist, he brought the yo-yo to a standstill. "But the Good Lord is very merciful, His love never ends. You have to know that Samuel prayed over you constantly, loved you deeply as well, and he wanted you to know where that love came from. But remember, the love of your master on earth was only a shadow of the love that your Master in heaven has for you...." Soon after he spoke those final words, he disappeared as sudden as he had come, the only sign that he had ever been there, being a carved staff on the ground.

    Taylor wrapped her arms around Yo-Yo's neck gently, comforting him as they both nuzzled against each other. Suddenly, his eyes darted around him as he whipped his neck back and forth, struggling to stand. Taylor's hands loosened around his neck as she stood up and looked around her as well. A line of people was stretching from where he and Taylor were standing; to as far back as he could see. What was happening here? The line wound around a ramshackle mercantile building, as people of all walks of life, dirty folk, proper gentlemen, small children, and even some of the gruff looking men in trench coats, but all of them poor and downtrodden, came one by one, up to the line. The man at the head of the line was the first to speak, thick tears rolling down his cheeks as he stretched out his hands to hand a rather large, wooden box to Taylor.

"We all have been discussing this since you arrived…we here aren't in any way wealthy, and have suffered just as much as the rest of the country. But, most of us are strong workers, and…well…we'd like to offer our services in whatever way we can, to help you rebuild this town and make it thrive. We've seen what you have meant to each other and how you have unselfishly given of what you have to us. Your examples have touched us in ways that we could never repay, without even knowing what you've done. We want to express our thanks and appreciation for showing us that, even though material things are important, it's the often overlooked things in life that mean the most of all. We have small, plain houses, nothing extravagant, but whenever you need them, they are yours. We have discovered that what we own and even our lives aren't really ours at all. We are truly grateful to God for what we have, you have shown us that. So now, all we possess is His, and by loving our neighbor, we show His grace, His love, and His mercy. Our time, our talents, our possessions, are yours. You can use what you need, when you need it."

Tears of both intense joy and extreme sadness streamed down Taylor's face as she gladly accepted the help and tools from the strangers, as one by one, they came with outstretched hands and full hearts. In a short amount of time, numerous tools, wrapped in cloth and leather lay behind her, as the citizens donated their services. She looked up toward heaven reverently with a grateful attitude of worship.

She smiled at the clouds streaming by, turning her face upwards further and stretching out her hands as the first, cool, steady drops of long awaited rain poured forth from the heavens. Slowly closing her eyes, she felt the drops become larger, as the ground soon was drenched in a flood. With the first rain in years hammering down upon them, the ground was soon saturated in a steady torrential downpour. One by one, they knelt slowly to the ground in the cool mud and breathed heartfelt prayers of thankfulness and blessing for all the Good Shepherd had given them. The men rushed to wrap blankets around the tools, so they wouldn't rust, and went back to surround Taylor, as they felt the cool, refreshing drops on their faces.

They briefly turned their heads when a middle aged woman in a worn apron, shouted Taylor's name over and over. Running up to them, out of breath, her hair plastered to her face, the muck reached her ankles. "Taylor, you're going to need to come quick... your sister is finally having her baby... I mean babies... Oh, Taylor, it's never been heard of, especially in these times! I've delivered many babies, some having triplets, but most of the people this happens to, it doesn't end well but... Now, listen to me, babbling like a brook... Guess what I mean to say is that... she's having triplets... oh my, it's been such a rough birth!" Taylor's hands shook as she covered her mouth, a smile once again covering her face as she whispered, "...Please, ma'am... I just need to know...what are the babies' names?" The woman knelt down closer, her face breaking into a wide smile, and she shouted above the downpour, "The first is named Cassidy, the name means 'clever', and I can tell, she is going to be a very clever girl indeed. It really is a miracle, they're all girls too! The other one is named Zoey; it's a Greek name meaning, 'life'! The last girl, oh, she's a unique one, she is! She's a cute girl with light blond hair! She is very active, always trying to smile...her name is Danae. Oh and they're all beautiful too, so very beautiful, look just like angels!"

You really *must* come see them sometime!" "Oh, I will!" Taylor promised. She hugged the woman tight as she sobbed. Soon, her hands aching, she fell to the ground as thick, unbidden tears of both intense joy and overwhelming sorrow streamed down her face. She simply folded her hands and closed her eyes, unaware of her dirtied clothes or the rain falling in sheets, soaking her to the bone. She stayed just like that for a long while, whispering over and over, "Thank you... Thank you so much...Thank you..." She was simply and fully aware that, in that moment, all of them, were safely sheltered in the Creator's loving and protective hand. The rest of the townspeople held hands, kneeling in the mud along with her, in deep adoration and worship. For they were now fully aware that nothing would ever be the same again, and no matter what events life brought their way, from now on, they truly would all live happily ever after.

The endless landscape burst into brilliance as a white, glorious light permeated everything. Samuel looked around him to see nothing but radiant, endless color. Swirls of the most beautiful hues rose and fell in rhythm, causing everything around him to shimmer. He rose to his feet slowly, taking in as much of it as he possibly could. Suddenly he felt a calm, soothing presence beside him. Turning to his right, a strong young man was walking with him. Their steps completely in rhythm, they began talking of things no mortal man could understand. As they walked past a crystal clear river, its surface as glass, Samuel was very much aware of where he was. He missed his loved ones; Taylor and Nathaniel. But he knew, clearer than he had ever known anything before, that this was where he was always meant to be, this was home, now and forevermore.

As he walked with the young man, he asked, "What will happen to Cassidy? And what of Boomerang?" The boy answered gently, but with authority, "You have lived a long, righteous life, believing in the One who gave you life. You deserve to know some things. Cassidy will have troubles come her way, many hardships; she's been raised well, but even I don't know if she can survive what lies ahead. As for Boomerang, he is a very special animal. Like the prophets of old, the Lord has given me a message. He will not see death until he has accomplished his purpose. The same holds true for his friend, Firebolt." They stopped at a grove of beautiful trees of all kinds, their branches bursting with the most amazing, colorful fruit imaginable. The young man stared at him through the most intense blue eyes he had ever seen; so full of compassion and acceptance. But Samuel's next question caused the young boy's eyes, though still kind and loving, to flash very briefly, with a frightening fire. Somewhere within those cobalt pools, a deep sadness and intense grief could also be felt, as tears slowly streamed down his cheeks.

"What happened to John, the sheriff? And what has become of Alex?", Samuel asked carefully.

"All you must know about that, is this: We all have to make decisions in life. John refused, or so he thought, to make a decision about his eternal destiny. But even the choice to remain undecided, is still a decision. There is coming a day we will all answer for the things we have done. The Lord is pleased that you have chosen wisely, my friend. As for Alex, his story will be revealed all in good time."

The boy spoke again softly to Samuel, his voice quiet, gentle and smooth, like a waterfall, "There has been much pain in your life, Samuel. There is so much that He wishes you didn't have to bear. But in the end it was all to bring Him glory. Surely you see that now. "

"Yes, I do.", Samuel said plainly, tears falling slowly down his face, as his eyes glued on the young man.

The boy reached up and placed a strong hand on Samuel's shoulder, his eyes bursting with more love than Samuel could possibly ever dream of. His next words, like all those before, were so pure and honest that Samuel thought surely he must be dreaming. This was by far the most real thing he had ever experienced! The boy spoke simply, his voice flowing from his mouth, yet ebbing and flowing from all around him as well, "Well done, good and faithful servant. Enter now into the joy of the crowning 'happily ever after'! Come and see the unfolding of the greatest fairy tale, the most joyous celebration, of which there shall never be any end!"

THE END

Epilogue: Early morning on December 7, 1941

More than a decade later, the townspeople gathered together to celebrate the rebirth of their town as well as their new found friendships. Nathaniel and Taylor were now a very elderly couple. After Samuel's death, Nathaniel made good on the promise he had made to Samuel during the fire. So, after falling in love, they started dating and got married a short while afterwards. Two full years, after the current mayor of the town had resigned; Nathaniel was unanimously elected as the next mayor of the town, being a reputable and honest man, like his friend Samuel before him. The regular term for past mayors had been four years, but the people voted to have him in office as long as he would like.

Nathaniel and Taylor sat in their rocking chairs, drinking lemonade, staring at the warm spring day outside their window, hand in hand, when a soft knock came at their door. Nathaniel sighed, leaned on his cane and pulled himself to his feet, hobbling to the door. Opening it, he noticed a strangely familiar face. The wrinkles of age were showing, his business suit was tattered and worn, and he had been clean shaven, but Nathaniel knew immediately who it was. With a worried look, his brow furrowed as a flood of memories came rushing back to him, memories of listening to stories of Samuel's long lost wife rushing back into his arms, and the stories of Samuel losing his only friend. He turned slowly to his wife. Her hands flew to her mouth in disbelief as tears came to her eyes.

After a long silence, it was Nathaniel who spoke next,

his words slow and methodical "We weren't sure we'd ever see you again around here, and I am truly ashamed to say, there were many days we hoped we never would. But now, in a strange way we can't explain, we're actually glad you came back. Time and events here have left us all changed, and in another time and place, before our eyes were opened, we would have turned you away. But things have happened here in the past that are bigger than all of us, and now we can do nothing less than let you inside as our guest. This doesn't mean we can forget everything you've done to my friend, my wife, and this town, but maybe we can at least try to forgive... and down the road, who knows? We may even become friends, but every journey does indeed begin with a single step", he said matter-of-fact. Taylor came from behind him, stepping closer, extending her hand, but still frowning.

    She whispered hoarsely, her voice choked with tears, "I have to admit, there are many horrible memories I would just as soon like to forget about, but at the same time, I can't deny, this place has changed me as well, I can't explain it, it is far more than anything we've done on our own... all I know is that, somehow, despite everything, I am ready and willing to forgive you." She paused for a moment, "Oh dear, I am afraid you must forgive me now, where are my manners? Please, please come in, if there is anything we can offer you, it is yours."

    Thick tears ran down the man's face as he took off his derby hat and cradled it in his hands, staring intently at it. He slowly stepped into the house, eternally thankful for this small act of courage and overwhelming kindness. Whispering hoarsely, tears flowed freely down his wrinkled cheeks.

    "Thank you, Taylor", Taylor's gaze softened as she

stared at him through thick tears. "You really have no idea what this means..." He let out a long, slow breath, as he began his confession. His eyes were downcast and his shoulders slumped. After years of playing games and refusing to see the truth, the wild animal had finally been caged, as he was forced to see his actions for what they were. "You see, I have had a long time to think on what kind of man I have become all these years. I had become a horrible, hate-filled person, convinced that I could never be good enough. When my parents died, I was taken to an orphanage and I realized I didn't fit in, I didn't belong there. So I ran away, set on making a life on my own. I rode the rails, going wherever the road took me. Most times I just spent the night there in them rail yards. Later in life, I got my hands on some books. I did me some learnin', studied hard and became a banker. I thought that would make me important, but I still had so much anger. I still wasn't satisfied with anything less than revenge. So that's when I found Samuel. At that point, I had convinced myself that he had a hand in my parent's death. So, I thought destroying him would make me happy, but in my quest, I became even more broken and bitter. Well, one thing led to another, and what you don't know is that, beginning that day so long ago, when you and Samuel held that service... I was there... and..."

Turning to Nathaniel, he spoke quietly, "I have some things I need to confess first. Remember your friend's journey to that saloon, and his card game to try and win that horse? I... was the one who planned the whole thing. The sheriff of the town was a good friend of mine, I told him before any of it started, to increase the stakes, knowing he would have to let go of the wedding ring to stay in the game. I was also the one who wrote that letter to him, telling him that Taylor had died. When I came to take his precious friend away, I acted like I was sorry for what I had to do. But, I wasn't. That was my plan all along. After the trip, me and John, the sheriff he won the horse from, we went to the cemetery and found a freshly dug grave. We put a cross on it, knowing that he would be by to see it every day. John carved Taylor's name on the cross, to complete the job. We wanted it to be a visual reminder of her, something he would have to see every day, but we had downright selfish reasons for doing so. Words can't express how sorry I am. I was gonna confess to the police right out, but I figured you needed to hear it first. I used to be a respected man, which I'm afraid to say, I ain't much of that no more. Well, I was afraid to go to the police and tell em of all I done. But I will, I promise. I was blinded by revenge, but I discovered that gets you nowhere. Being a man means facing up to what you got comin' to ya, even when you know it'll hurt."

    I am sure he had been by what you thought to be her grave, many times. Thing is, his last name was 'Phillips'. When he was told Taylor had died, he couldn't do anything about it, since he was attacked in the alley. The man who attacked him, he sent a message to a friend of his, once he knew he wouldn't be gettin' up fer a while. He put in that letter that I had put a drug into her, something that would kill her. It didn't kill her. I suppose it knocked her out for a while, but she was up on her feet again after a couple days.

    Once Samuel came to, he'd read the letter and, we knew it would leave him devastated and broken. We didn't count on his persistence, we figured he would just lose faith and... I dunno. I suppose love really is stronger than death. That there grave he always went by, that was someone with the last name of 'Phillips', but it was a distant relative, too distant to make a difference. Apparently, whoever took the record, wrote down the wrong information. You always thought he was going to see Taylor, but he wasn't. It took a while for us to get out of England; we had to lay low after what we had done, the kidnapping and all...

Ten years or so, before that fateful day that began this whole horrible mess, I became a banker in the nearest town. I worked hard and, when the day came to finally have my revenge, me and the sheriff, placed a cross on a grave near where he lived, and wrote Taylor's name on it. We knew that if he saw her first name that would make it real for him. So we wrote it in big letters, so he could find it easily. From then on, the whole betrayal began." Alex's head turned to Samuel at that instant, his gaze boring into his friend's, his next words full of icy, cold rage, "When my parents died, I was so broken. I thought my life was ending. The world I had known was gone. They were my rock, my anchor. And then, I looked closer... and I saw your friend running behind him! At first I thought he might be trying to catch the thief, but then I noticed, the way that he walked wasn't like someone who was in pursuit! He had Samuel's shirt on too! I didn't know what to think, but then all the pieces seemed to fit right in. In my anger, I realized then that your dear friend was in on the whole thing! He had SOMETHING to do with it! I don't know what it is, but I will find out, and when I do, I will come for you! He is already gone, but I can still destroy you! I came for everything else he held dear, and I refuse to rest until I destroy you too!"

Samuel held his hands up in protest, "Wait a minute, now! Think about what yer sayin'! Samuel was there that night your parent's died, but he was honestly tryin' to catch the thief! You and him have been friends for so long, you're accusing him of this now, after he's gone and can't defend himself? Listen, he told me, he heard the gunshot, but the reason he didn't come running is cause he had suffered a lot of grief! I know that doesn't make sense, but in his sadness, he heard the gunshot, but he didn't put the two together! When you're so focused on yourself, you have a hard time seeing the things around you… he would have been there, really he would have, but it's just… Ok, I'll tell you what. Maybe this will explain things." He hung his head and from his pocket, he slowly pulled a leather strap. Hanging from the strap was a crucifix. Alex's eyes widened, as he trembled. "He doesn't own this. We've been through each other's belongings many times! We worked together! Where did you get it from?" Nathaniel's eyes softened as he spoke, "He told me that he got this from a shop overseas, when he took that trip. While he was there, your goons attacked him and threw the letter in a puddle beside him, knowing he would read it when he awoke."

"Yes, I remember." Samuel frowned.

Samuel continued, "Before he…well, you know… he saw the thief under a bridge. He told me that he just figured he was a homeless person. He didn't think anything of it at the time. The man had a knife tucked in his clothes, but he told Samuel it was for eating, when he found scraps. Samuel trusted him; he would believe anything you told him, that's how trusting he was. But he couldn't just let him go with nothing. So he pulled out the leather crucifix he had bought. He told me all this firsthand, one day, so I know it to be true. He didn't count on you accusing him of anything, especially now. He just wanted me to know what really happened. Even though he trusted him, he had a feeling the knife was for more than eating, but couldn't prove anything. So he gave the thief the cross and told him to just keep it. The thief needed it more than he did, I figured. Anyways, your parents dying and Samuel being attacked was around the same time. So, next thing he knew, he was lying face-down in an alley, and that note was beside him. When he came to, the leather strap was lying beside him as well, in a puddle. When he was able to regain enough consciousness to think plainly, he just figured the thief, in his anger, had tossed it aside and wasn't gonna have any more to do with it. So you see… Samuel had nothing to do with your grief. He was just trying, in his own way, to offer help. You say you saw the man with one of Samuel's shirts on. Well, when he gave him that cross, he also gave him one of the shirts that he had too. It seemed like the right thing to do. All I can say is that I am sorry that you feel the way you do. But that is my story, and I ain't changing the truth." Alex's head drooped further as he realized the full truth, "So, you had nothing to do with it?"

"You know me, Alex, I'm an honest man. I learned a lot from Samuel during this short time. Think about it, please. All those years you and him were workin' together… would he really do something like that to you?"

Alex's eyes fixed on the floor, refusing to meet Samuel's gaze, as he very slowly spoke, his words coming slow and thoughtful. "You're right... I guess I was blinded by my rage. Anyways, I am so very sorry… Making him believe a lie is the most horrible, terrible thing I have ever done. I just wanted to find hope and

Kyle Nathan Buller

meaning, and if I couldn't, I promised myself no one else would either. I realize it's no excuse, I see that now. I was just angry, so very angry...But, as I was saying, I was there when you held that service all those years ago, and I don't know what happened, or how, or even why, but" with his next words, his voice cracked and he could barely go on, "my life started to changed again, eventually. Oh, I still had many questions. But I found true hope and real meaning, what I had been searching for my whole life. I was with a young boy in England when you went there to visit your cousin. You might remember walking with him. Anyway, you handed him a Bible. At first, he said no. But he took it later on, after my friend beat you up in the alley, and handed it to me. I kept it so I could find out more about this hope you have in you. I figured that maybe I could find an argument against this God you claim to believe in. I did not have good intentions at all. But the more I read it, the more I realized that the book I had in my hands was really a letter, a love letter it seemed had been written just for me." He held the Bible softly in his hands, rubbing his fingers over the worn, raised lettering. He let out a long, slow sigh and continued.

In that moment, he let out a whistle and a familiar black stallion trotted up to the window. Alex continued, as he wrapped his hands around the reins, "I took this horse the day I had the argument with Taylor in the farmhouse, right before you two got reunited. I guess I figured that Samuel was comin' no matter what I did, and so I took the horses as a last resort. I guess knowin' he was comin' to rescue you got me thinkin'. I was too proud to admit it at the time, but something inside me started changin'. I was jealous for someone to love me the way Taylor obviously loved, and I'm guessin', still loves, Samuel. I thought long and hard, and I knew I needed rescuin' too. I took them horses, and it was risky, but I stayed behind long enough to see you too reunited. I nearly broke down at the sight, but still I was stubborn. I did what I had to do. I made my way to Chicago here, same route as you, only through another tunnel. When I got here, I made sure no one would recognize me. Changed my name, shaved got glasses and did what I could." I expected a different life, but with being a banker I should have known better. This place been hit as hard as the rest of the country. I was forced to stand in bread lines and take up shelter in these places", Alex said, pointing to one of the Hoovervilles. I guess that just made me realize that with all the fightin' I been doin' to keep what I got and all, it wasn't amounting to much. My search for vengeance was making me a monster. Made me terribly ashamed to be standin' in those lines, and I hung my head down low. I didn't want anyone to see me, I knew what they might be thinking... but I still didn't want you to see me either. Even in my hard times, I still was a terrible person. Oh, I coulda had all the money in the world and none of it woulda satisfied me. It took Samuel's words to help me realize my huge mistake. I needed something more. My life was outta control. Remember... remember when Samuel went on that trip to England? He took a freighter, was gonna go visit his sister? While he was there, this young boy came up to him and struck up a conversation, and he tried to give him a Bible? You remember any of that?"

"Yes, I remember... His name was William, if I remember right..." Nathaniel said thoughtfully.

Alex continued slowly, staring at the floor. "Well, the reason he was actin' all friendly toward you is... I asked him to. I got him to follow you and once he got what I asked him for, he reported back to me and, it was a terrible thing he did. But I put him up to it, and you have to know that, he wasn't always like that. That day, long ago, when I drugged your wife and was caught tryin' to escape, it was that same little boy, who rushed over and saw something was wrong. He reported what he saw and, well, he came with a policeman to arrest me. There was a gunfight, and the policeman... I didn't mean for this to happen but, I crippled him." He closed his mouth, balling his hands into tight fists, tears streaming down his face. After he had wiped away the tears with the back of his hand, he just sat there, remaining silent for awhile, before speaking once again, "They put me in prison, where I belong, and that's where I been all this time. I owe William a debt of gratitude, actually. Being in prison has let me think about things. I got off on good behavior to come here and confess to you, but I ain't finished my sentence. I have many years left. I know I done wrong, I'm trying to make things as right as I can. You deserve to know the truth and whatever happens from now on, somehow, the truth is gonna make me free."

    Nathaniel heard all that Alex was saying, but right now, his eyes were focused on Malice. He spoke with authority to the horse, but the words he spoke next, were for Alex as well. Nathaniel continued to look on curiously as he remembered Samuel telling of his short adventures with this bad-tempered animal. But then he had remembered the way the sheriff had treated this poor animal and Samuel felt sorry for him. He still was forced to let him go after the rescue of the calf, due to Malice's injuries and dark mood. Nathaniel took the reins of Malice and whispered, hoping Alex would hear as well,

"Samuel told me before he died, how much of a problem you were. I know that the sheriff was all you knew. You had no choice but to follow the only example you had ever known. But now things are different. I'm not sure where John is anymore, I suppose he got lost in the dust storms or had something worse happen to him. So now, it's time you have a new start. You deserve a new beginning and I know just the place for you... Wait right here, till me and Alex finish talkin' and I'll get ya set up good and proper."

Nathaniel took his hands from Malice's reins and placed them on his hips. Alex's face darkened further as he continued his confession, "The figure you saw going into the hotel after the revival, shortly before the fire, that... was me." His head sunk lower in shame, wishing for the floor to swallow him whole. "I started that fire. I heard your message; I just wasn't ready to accept it at the time. I went inside, and messed around with the wires. As a child, I read up on books about electricity, so I knew how to do that kind of thing. I worked it out, so as soon as Taylor turned on the lights, the circuits would short out and the fire would start. To be honest, I felt like Judas, the disciple who betrayed Jesus. So I guess I figured I should play the part I thought I was meant to play. I burned that hotel down. And I am here because I need to ask for your forgiveness. I've had time to think about what I had done, after it was all over and my punishment had been served. One night, guilt began consuming me and I nearly reached the end of my rope. But then, my mind went back to that awful moment after I took Yo-Yo away, and I replayed every moment leading up to it, over in my mind. It was like a light had switched on in my heart. I accepted what my parents had tried to teach me all along and I know now that I was so very wrong…Can you ever forgive me for all the horrible, terrible things I've done to you?" There have been moments I have seemed sorry for my actions, and at the time, I honestly thought I was. But I realize those were just motions I was going through. Now I realize the consequences and am begging for your forgiveness."

Taylor and Nathaniel hesitated before answering, allowing Alex one final plea on his behalf. "Remember long ago, Taylor, when I kidnapped you and held you in my apartment? I recounted to you what was going to happen, and knowing how much you enjoyed fairy tales as a child, I related my plans to you, in that sort of analogy. And this is the reason." At that moment, Alex brought forth a worn book of fairy tales!" Taylor wept as memories of her mother reading to her, washed over her. How she longed for the days when she would sit in her mother's lap and have those stories read to her! She missed her dear mother, Sarah, so very much! He handed the book to Taylor and continued, as she clutched it tightly to her chest. "I told you that I had played the part of the dragon, and every dragon's most vulnerable point is his heart. I knew I'd be in trouble for what I was doing, and I had to take him down with me. I thought I needed to rain down my destruction on your poor Samuel, but it wasn't him who deserved that punishment. He didn't do nothing wrong. He just told people the truth of God's love, same way I did.

When my parents died, I needed someone to lash out at. I had abandoned God, but He never has given up on me. I guess what I'm saying is I'm the one that deserves punishment. So if you would be so kind, call the authorities now and have em take me away, it's what I deserve... I'll confess to everything. I only gave em part of the truth, but they deserve to hear it all too." He whispered one final thing, "I remember you saying then that I needed a change of heart. I laughed your comment off at first, but I never forgot what you had said. Little did I know how true it was..."

Nathaniel and Taylor stood before him, listening, as her sister entered the room, a fairly tall, energetic dark-haired girl bouncing playfully beside her, holding a yo-yo. At twelve years old, she was very mature for her age, and very outspoken. Taylor's sister, running to keep pace, came from beside the little girl. She stared at Alex curiously for the longest time before asking, "Her name is Cassidy, would you like to go outside and play, maybe teach her how to use the toy?" A warm smile of relief broke across his face as he whispered, "Yes, yes I would, very much! Taylor leaned forward and whispered gently to Cassidy, "Could you just let me and Alex talk for a minute? He'll be right out afterward."

"I suppose, that's ok..." Cassidy looked down at her feet in disappointment, but walked a few feet away and played quietly. Taylor stared seriously at Alex, her arms folded across her chest, "We're not gonna report you to the authorities. See, my husband, he's the mayor around here, has been for a while now, and I believe he has something he wants to say to you about that. Samuel spoke next in a very serious tone, his words very solemn. "I am indeed the mayor around here, and I could have you punished severely for what you done. But you've had enough punishment, like I already said."

"So, aside from not arresting you, I am gonna make you my assistant, if you'll have the job. I need a righteous, upstanding man to fill the position. Now, we all know you done wrong, but you made a heartfelt, sincere apology, and you're forgiven. I need you to prove to me and this town, that you learned your lesson. Don't let us down, Alex, we're counting on you. I'll be sure to keep a good eye on you at all times. I'm allowing the rest of this town to do the same thing. They'll be my spies. We aren't trying to be mean; we just gotta keep you accountable, you understand. You'll serve the rest of your sentence here. We were the victims of your crimes; I think that the law will let us keep an eye on you. Now understand, it's not going to be easy; it will be a long, difficult process to trust you again. But since you will be my assistant, I need to be able to trust you. I've given these citizens the right to turn you in if you mess up. You've done things; things that will make us question you for a long time. But we forgive you; we've been forgiven, beautifully flawed as we are, so it only makes sense to return the favor. You don't deserve it, but then again, neither did we deserve what Christ did for us.

You need to understand something else, the difference between mercy and grace. Grace is saying, 'I am taking away the punishment you deserve' and mercy is giving you something you don't deserve. You should rightly be punished, but you've probably had plenty of time to think these past few years. With all the thinking you've done, you've no doubt had time to come to your senses. So, in that respect, you're guilty, havin' to play your crime over and over in your mind. But, like I said, you're free to go. We ain't gonna make you go back to a cell. All you gotta do is promise to never go down that far ever again, and make good on your promise. We all make mistakes; it's what we learn from our mistakes that makes all the difference. No, we decided that instead, we're graciously inviting you inside our home for a meal. Never forget this lesson." Alex smiled nervously as he nodded in understanding. Cassidy asked him one last, final question, before drawing the confession to an end, "Before we go in for the meal, I just would like to know one last thing. What made you confess all this now? What brought you out of your madness? Oh, we believe you when you say you discovered the Lord, but.... what was it that brought that on?"

Alex stared at the floor and began to speak. "When I was in prison, a church nearby had a ministry. Different people came and talked to us about what they been through, hopin' to inspire us and all. One day, a man named James Braddock came and spoke to us. He would become the heavyweight champion, I'd come to find out later. He came walkin' in... nice clean suit and all, looking all proper. Anyways, he was born in a very rough part of New York City. He took up boxing and lost a fight for the championship, severely injuring his hand. It was a narrow loss, he almost won that fight. His family became poor during the Depression and he was forced to work on the docks, like many of us. Because of the injuries to the hand he was usin' all the time, he worked with his other hand, making it stronger. He was humiliated just like I was, accepting handouts from bread lines and such, but he heard about an organization that was helping people that were homeless and down on their luck. He managed to give back all the money that he got from the government and started giving money to the places he had heard about. He even invited homeless people to eat dinner with him.

Well, I started looking into some of the places he gave money to, and they were good Christian places. I looked some more into what they do, got my hands on some of the fliers and all, that they put out. Samuel, when you and I worked together, I heard that same stuff day after day, but it just made me angrier and angrier. Now I see that wasn't the point. Those fliers said that God reveals himself to us, not to shame us, but to make us better than we were before. I suppose that before I went to prison, I had known of God, but I didn't really know Him. It's strange how two people can look at the same thing and notice something different. We both saw the Gospel. But where you saw grace and mercy, I saw in it, power and control over people. Anyway, when James came to visit, I figured that if he could make a better life for himself, and make an example to others, then so could I. But it starts with confessin' what I done, and well, here I am." Nathaniel and Taylor smiled, knowing that their friend was finally beginning to understand. Taylor leaned toward Nathaniel and whispered, "I think it's finally time...."

"Time for what?", asked Alex.

Nathaniel stared at Alex, and replied, "This is something I think you are finally ready for. I want you to kneel, Alex." Alex slowly knelt to the ground, with his face turned down, as Nathaniel took a sword from its place on the wall. "This belonged to my father. He was a soldier during World War I. He lost it during the war. He was killed, but it was recently found a short distance from where he lay. Since I was the only living member of his family, it is in my possession now." As his fingers wrapped around the gilded hilt, Taylor interrupted, holding forth the book of fairy tales. "You told me once that I was a princess and you were the dragon, and I needed a prince to come rescue me. Well, I've found my prince. You were partly right in what you said. All of our lives have the possibility of happy endings. But, if we try to create our own stories, with our own pens, any peace we find in that can only last for a short while. The only lasting happy ending is one found in Christ, let Him write your story. Never forget that, Alex."

Next, Nathaniel lowered the sword, blade down, to each of Alex's shoulders. "I hereby appoint you my assistant as mayor of this here town. My friend, he was teased very harshly when he was younger. So he started thinkin' that his faith amounted to nothin' more than fairy tales. It was all the bullies' fault, it was. But I do believe our experiences have taught us that God is so more than just a fairy tale. He's more real than you'll ever imagine, more real than I'm lookin' at you right now, in fact. All we've seen and been a part of lately, is sorta like a fairy tale. So, I guess it only made sense to knight you. After all, we're all soldiers of Christ. The book of Ephesians speaks of being clothed with the armor of a knight, does it not?" Alex rose slowly, his eyes never wavering from Nathaniel, as a flood of pure, deep love, acceptance, and forgiveness seemed to flow from the man. Alex slowly nodded in agreement, taking Nathaniel's hand and shaking it gratefully, his eyes welling with tears. Kneeling down, he turned eagerly to Cassidy, wiping his eyes, "While I teach you how to use it, would you like to hear a story that a dear friend told me once, about the yo-yo? It's sort of a magical tale." Cassidy replied with a resounding, "Oh yes, please, sir!" as her eyes widened.

Nathaniel and Taylor looked in each other's eyes, smiling, as Alex took Cassidy's hand. Then they whispered to one another, as Nathaniel reached his other hand out to Taylor. Both his hands in hers, they smiled uncontrollably, whispering, "Yes, I think we know exactly what this means....to us all. It means renewed hope, it means a new beginning, and, above all, it means return."

An hour later, tied securely to a wooden post in front of the firehouse across town, grazing on a fresh pile of hay, three horses whinnied contentedly; a deep brown stallion with a perfect circle on his forehead, as well as a majestic white stallion. Finally, a strong black stallion played in the distance as he threw his head back and forth in amusement. Two men leaned against the fence, staring at them. The strong, handsome young man, named William, said to his partner, "I remember years ago, I was in England, as a young boy. The land over yonder is just like here," he said, motioning to the peaceful, serene field. "A long while after that run in with Alex and his men, my aunt died quite unexpectedly. I had no family left, they all died from disease, and God bless 'em. So, I was brought to America here, and I took up odd jobs on farms, going from town to town. Well, I came across Samuel later in my life, and I he told me how he just lost his horse. Was set on goin' into town to get another one, he was. I wished him luck, and went back to finding work. I had this strange feeling though that somehow, our paths would cross again, and well, here we are."

They heard a loud snort as a midnight black horse, bucked up and down playfully, tossing his head as his mane flew behind him in the wind. They turned their heads, William saying to his friend, "I do believe that black horse is the most playful horse we ever did see! He used to belong to that sheriff back in Nebraska, his reputation preceded him, and everyone knew he was a mean old pest, that one. But ever since Malice was brought here, it seems to us like something's changed in him... He ain't nothing like he used to be." William vaulted the fence and walked over to Malice. Kneeling down, he noticed a large curved upside down 'V' on its hindquarters. Raising himself up, he stretched out his hands, laid them on Malice's face, staring intently at the horse. "You used to be named Malice, a cruel name if I say so myself. But since you came here, you deserve a new name, something fitting of your new personality and your journey. We're gonna call ya Boomerang. It also means, 'return', just like your friend over yonder," as he nodded to Yo-Yo. He took his hands away from Boomerang's face and walking up a slight hill, knelt down, laying in the cool grass, staring at the clouds. They all breathed deeply of the fresh, clean air, as they relaxed for a long while.

A short distance away, underneath the shade of a miniature cluster of trees; a single stone marker pronounced its lone occupant, 'Here lies Samuel, friend of the oppressed, lover of the Most High God, champion of the weak.' A moment of solemn silence ensued as they respectfully stared at the grave, then the two men stood up. Turning their heads in the direction of the trees, William said to his friend, "All of these trees here mean something. We chose that there oak tree to bury Samuel, because it's a symbol of strength and courage, and Lord knows that Samuel had enough of that to go around. I heard it's also a symbol of the faithfulness between a man and wife, that's very fittin' because he loved his dear Taylor more than life itself. It'll grow up big and strong and shade us for years to come. That one there in the distance is an apple tree. An apple tree signifies magic, like in that book of fairy tales that's buried with Taylor. Their lives weren't perfect, but they did have a happy ending', William said, remembering the service held in there in the town square, years ago. The other man nodded solemnly "Before he was buried, Taylor insisted we bury Samuel with that book of fairy tales. She fought hard for the right to put it there herself, she did. Must've been special to her, I suppose. The happy ending that Samuel gave us is better thought than any fairy tale you could tell, cause we serve a risen Savior. Now there's also a birch tree, just to the left there". William added. "It's symbolic of all of us. It stands for new beginnings and cleansing of the past, what we've experienced in Christ. To the far right over there, that's a Cherry tree, symbolic of death and rebirth, also an example of what Christ did for us.

"Just behind that one is a cypress tree, a symbol of sacrifice. Before Samuel died from the smoke inhalation, he risked everything to tell us all about Jesus. Those big burly men with them big guns we seen walking around, they was part of the Mafia. They think they can just come in here and be the law, well, they ain't. Anyways, as Samuel was preachin', those men come and just stood in the background, holding their weapons. We were certain that we was just waitin' to be shot, they don't take kindly at all to the gospel, same as Alex used to, but I guess we were protected somehow. They seen us, but never moved a muscle. Guess something scared em stiff. Suppose you could say that was a sacrifice in itself, what he done fer us. Now then, behind that is a holly tree. We'll use the berries come Christmastime. Holly trees are symbolic of overcoming anger, protection and being a spiritual warrior. To face all that Samuel faced, he had to have protection and he was for sure a spiritual warrior. As for overcoming anger, Samuel had plenty of reasons, more than any of us, to be angry, but his faith never wavered. Let that be a lesson to all of us. Let Yo-Yo's determination and obedience and innocence be a example for us all as well."

    They looked on respectfully and smiled as they leaned on the fence. As they stood in silence, they were admiring the scene and remembering all that had been done for them. "The entire town came together to plan and attend to the funeral, an act of unselfish brotherhood in a time of selfish uncertainty. And then this happened.", William said, motioning to the trees. They just up and grew here, no explanation at all. It's a miracle, is what it is. What's even more of a miracle, is that not a single one of these trees are supposed to be growing here. The weather, the soil, they ain't supposed to be good for em. One of the men in town, an expert on trees, actually, figured out what they all mean and they are all a tribute to poor Samuel. God knows what we needed to honor Samuel's memory and He provided. The prophet Jeremiah in the Bible talks about strong trees planted by streams of water. Just behind this grove is a river," he pointed in the distance to a lazy river, winding through the trees, the sun reflecting its rays off the surface like diamonds. "They ain't terribly tall, but the fact that they're here at all is indeed a miracle, no other way to say it." William and the other man stared thoughtfully to the river, through the trees, then back down at the grave, their minds and hearts thinking on these things, yet full of gratitude.

    The two men walked slowly back to Boomerang, and the horse with the perfect circle on his forehead. As they watched the three horses playing enthusiastically, William said to his friend, "There's something I been meaning to show ya." He carefully pulled a folded piece of yellowed paper from the pocket of his overalls. "This here come from my grandfather. Seems like this whole journey has been about one thing, hope. Oh, faith and love, most definitely. But, more than anything, hope. Samuel told me all about his journey to get here, what Alex done to him and all, and, there's no denyin' it's about hope." His friend nodded as he clapped him on the back, agreeing wholeheartedly. "Now, this here is a letter my grandpa wrote during the war, near the end. He wrote it to his fiance overseas, seems like a fitting end to this whole story, I should think." Unfolding the letter slowly, he put on his reading glasses. He cleared his throat and began to read, his voice shaking with sadness, "My dearest Sarah..."

As he finished reading the letter, the sun shone through the thin paper, causing William to exclaim, "Hey, now wait a minute, I do believe there's something written on the back side of this letter. I've had it for years and I just now seen it. Can't understand how I could have missed it." Turning it over in his hands, he began reading the remainder of the letter, written in a smooth, patient, flowing script:

P.S. It is now two days later from the time I first began writing this letter to you, my dear Sarah. I am sitting in a farmhouse in the French town of Compiegne. A farmer has agreed to let us use his home as a temporary settlement for our troops, provided we do chores for him, which we are more than happy to do. My men are now outside talking or working or some such thing, while I sit inside finishing writing this long overdue letter. I do not know how long it will take, but my promise still holds true that somehow, I shall return to you, in due time. There is much left to be done, in the meanwhile.

My mind can't help but return to just days earlier, when I met Cyrus. The Lord alone must have known I needed a horse. He knew also that I cared deeply for my bride, and was desperate to be back with you. He also must have known I couldn't do it without the help and support of my men. For that, I am truly grateful. I leave you now with this parting thought of comfort. Storms will surely come in our lives. I have no idea when this war shall end, but I pray it comes quickly, God willing. When these storms do come our way, God always uses them for His purpose. We may not always see it, and it may be painful, but I can say most assuredly, that with the support of our friends, and with the aid of God Almighty, we shall come through on the other side. Our one and only job, when uncertainty comes, is to trust in His promises, praise Him within the storms, and stand back as He displays His might. Enclosed, I have included the words to an old forgotten hymn that I pray gives you comfort until I see you once again. I love you with all my heart, my dear Sarah.

Though troubles assail/And dangers affright
Though friends should all fail/And foes all unite
Yet one thing secures us/Whatever betide
The scripture assures us/The Lord will provide
The birds, without barn/Or storehouse are fed
From them let us learn/To trust for our bread
His saints what is fitting/Shall never be denied
So long as 'tis written/The Lord will provide
His call we obey/Like Abraham of old
Not knowing our way/But faith makes us bold
For though we are strangers/We have a good Guide
And trust in all dangers/The Lord will provide
When Satan appears/to stop up our path

*And fill us with fears/We triumph by faith
He cannot take from us/Though oft he has tried
The heart-cheering promise/The Lord will provide
He tells us we're weak/Our hope is in vain
The good that we seek/We never shall obtain
But when such suggestions/Our faith thus have tried
This answers all questions/The Lord will provide
No strength of our own/Nor goodness we claim
Our trust is all thrown/On Jesus' dear name
In this our strong tower/For safety we hide
The Lord is our power/The Lord will provide
When life sinks apace/And death is in view
The word of His grace/Shall comfort us through
Not fearing or doubting/With Christ on our side
We hope to die shouting/The Lord will provide!*

After the man had finished reading the letter, they placed their arms against the fence, staring out at the scene, as the sun's rays cast shadows over the landscape, in a beautiful symphony of colors. The two men looked up slowly to the sky, as a soft whine in the distance grew to a rapid, earsplitting roar of engines. Seven fighter planes flew by in attack formation, very close and low to the ground, as the deafening noise drowned out the playful cries of the three horses. As William and his friend looked on in disbelief, the suns rays caught one of the planes' insignias, as it banked to the right, showing a large red circle with red rays streaming forth from it, against a field of white; the emblem of Japan's fleet! Both men looked on in horror, as the three horses stopped their playing, staring curiously into the sky, sensing the tension. They had heard rumors that this may happen, but now it was becoming stark reality; no longer a spectator, the United States was now suddenly been forced to enter

World War II! The land of the free and home of the brave was on the verge of being officially attacked!

Credit and References Page

Acts 4:32-37 (The Believers Share Their Possessions)
32 All the believers were one in heart and mind. No one claimed that any of their possessions was their own, but they shared everything they had. *33* With great power the apostles continued to testify to the resurrection of the Lord Jesus. And God's grace was so powerfully at work in them all *34* that there were no needy persons among them. For from time to time those who owned land or houses sold them, brought the money from the sales *35* and put it at the apostles' feet, and it was distributed to anyone who had need.

Jeremiah 29:11
11 For I know the plans I have for you," declares the LORD, "plans to prosper you and not to harm you, plans to give you hope and a future.

Proverbs 11:28
28 Those who trust in their riches will fall,
But the righteous will thrive like a green leaf

Deuteronomy 32:10-12
10 In a desert land he found him,
In a barren and howling waste.
He shielded him and cared for him;
He guarded him as the apple of his eye,
11 Like an eagle that stirs up its nest
And hovers over its young and carries them aloft.
12 The LORD alone led him;
No foreign god was with him.

Jeremiah 17:8
8 They will be like a tree planted by the water
That sends out its roots by the stream
It does not fear when heat comes
Its leaves are always green.
It has no worries in a year of drought
And never fails to bear fruit."

Psalm 33:17-19
17 A horse is a vain hope for deliverance;
Despite all its great strength it cannot save.
18 But the eyes of the LORD are on those who fear him,
On those whose hope is in his unfailing love,
19 To deliver them from death and keep them alive in famine.

Copyright © 1973, 1978, 1984, 2011 by Biblica
All references concerning using banana oil mixed with grain to serve as a fertilizer for defense against grasshoppers, are contributed to my late grandfather, Dean D. Buller, of Henderson, Nebraska
yo-yo *[yo -yo] n (plural yo-yos)* 1. toy with string wound on spool: a toy consisting of a long string wound onto a spool that is dropped and raised repeatedly using the force of gravity and momentum to unwind and rewind the string 2. fluctuating thing: something that repeatedly goes up and down or fluctuates between one extreme and another (**Encarta ® World English Dictionary © & (P) 1998-2005 Microsoft Corporation.** *All rights reserved.*)
(*All Bible verses taken from the New International Version*) **Though Troubles Assail** and **How Great Thou Art** hymn lyrics taken from www.lyricsondemand.com

Kyle Nathan Buller

Made in the USA
Lexington, KY
17 July 2017